Date-ABILITY

Young Single Austens

WS Deming

Little Gray House

Little Gray House

Dedication

To my sisters, who always had my back

contents

CHaPTer 1

Abby inspected her look in her bedroom mirror. The knee-length skirt she'd found at Deseret Industries complimented her legs—not to mention the new heels she'd found at the same time. She popped her foot up. Heels—her favorite thing.

"Are you almost ready to go?" Sara called from the front room of their house. Her older sister was a stickler for being on time for church.

"Yes, I'm coming," Abby said. She smoothed her skirt down and turned one more time to inspect the back. She sighed, lamenting that she hadn't gotten Sara and her mother's tiny figure. She didn't like that her back and front end stuck out a little too much for her comfort, and even though Sara insisted Abby was shapely, everyone knew what that really meant.

She walked into the front room of their little rented house. Sara looked adorable as usual in her simple maxi dress. Their cousin, Crystal, had shortened it so it wouldn't get caught in Sara's wheelchair wheels, and the dress's lines gave Sara a delicate, feminine look. It also didn't hurt that she had creamy, pale skin and gorgeous dark red hair that went past her shoulders. Abby's hair was a drab dishwasher blonde that she lightened to a bright blonde just to keep up.

One thing Abby had going for her was her wicked sense of style. That was something Sara really didn't care about. Abby loved clothes—the less expensive (and more stylish) the better. She just couldn't afford much, being in school full time. Before they died, her parents had managed to put together a trust for her and her sister, and they survived on the small payment it provided.

"I'll drive," Sara said. "Does Will want us to pick him up again?"

"I don't know," Abby said, thinking of her gorgeous best friend. It took a lot for her not sigh. "I'll text him and see if he's even coming to church at all."

She pulled her phone out and sent the message. Abby had known Will since high school. Meeting him reminded her of a scene from one of those cheesy teen romance movies—he came strutting into her English class, like a beach bum god with his blonde mass of loose curly hair and baby blue eyes, and sat down right next to her. He dazzled her with a brilliant dimpled smile and flirtingly teased her the whole rest of class. At the time, she'd been in heaven thinking that maybe this beautiful specimen was interested in her but she quickly found that he was like that with all the girls he came in contact with. But she couldn't help herself. She made sure they were friends and tortured herself all three years of high school being the friend, but never the girlfriend.

Not much had changed since they graduated. She'd moved on to college and he moved on to working full time. He still texted her nearly every day. He took her with him to do stuff when he didn't have a girlfriend, but beyond that he'd never given her any hope there was more to it than that. Still, she always secretly held onto the hope that one day things would change.

Her phone buzzed.

Yeah, come get me.

"He says yes," Abby said, more excited than she should be.

Sara rolled her eyes. "Then we better get going so we won't be late. Hopefully he's already ready. Tell him we won't wait for him to powder his nose."

Sara didn't like Will. She tolerated him because he was Abby's friend, and because she knew her sister was in love with him. But she didn't like the way he treated Abby, as some back-burner girlfriend. She felt her sister deserved better. The argument of a thousand days was old and she wished Sara would leave it alone. Will was capable of giving her what she wanted . . . he just needed to see it himself.

"I wonder if the weirdo will be there today." Abby said as they drove to Will's house.

"The weirdo?"

"Yeah, the new guy, you know? The tall one with brown hair and beard. I always catch him staring at me."

"Maybe he likes you," Sara said.

"Too bad for him, then. He's not my type."

"He's not that bad looking."

"Then you date him."

"But he's not looking at me," Sara said. Abby heard her mutter, "They never are."

"Sara, you're too beautiful to be single forever."

"Yeah, but I'm disabled enough to be single forever."

"You don't know that."

"I'm twenty-one years old, Abby, and I've only been on one date and that's because I asked him," Sara said. "Doesn't matter. I'm nearly done with school. Apply to teach art somewhere, and give violin lessons in my spare time. I'll be sitting right here in Riverton so you have someplace to come home to when you're off being a pharmacist."

Abby looked at her sister. Sara tried looking outwardly strong but Abby knew Sara's brave front masked the worry that she never seemed to catch anyone's eye. That was something the two sisters had in common. Neither one had dated much—Sara because of her wheelchair and Abby because of her weight. No one wanted to date the "curvy" girl either. It seemed to affect Sara more than it did Abby. Sara wanted all the things anyone else wanted—a family of her own, particularly children.

Abby wasn't in a hurry for any of that. She was barely through the first year of college and she had at least seven more to go. Now if Will were to make himself available then maybe she'd consider marriage and family a little earlier. Other than him, she wasn't in a rage to do anything but school. A relationship would slow things down. But it would be nice to know that someone admired her, thought her beautiful and told her so, and just have someone to do fun things with on a Friday night—or even just snuggle.

They pulled up to Will's house and he jumped in the back.

"Ladies," he said, with his rakish grin.

"Will," Sara said. "Thank you for not making us wait."

"Sara, only for you," he said. All he got from Sara was a tight smile. Will's charms did not work on Sara—at all. "Abby, are we going to the mall on Tuesday?"

"Why? So you can torture me with all the clothes I can't afford?" Abby asked.

"I'm bored and I need new jeans," Will said. "They're making me work tomorrow at the call center but I can go on Tuesday. Come with me, please?"

Abby really wanted to say no. She should drag him off to the Draper DI. She hadn't been there in a while and if she was lucky, she could find a few designer labels in her size. But knowing Will, he'd turn his nose up at wearing second-hand. Looking into his sparkling baby blues, she knew she'd say yes. So did he.

"Fine, I get out of school at three Tuesday afternoon," she said. "I'm assuming I'm picking up your lazy butt?"

"Would you? You'd be my BFF," he said.

"I already am," she said, rolling her eyes, but she smiled at him.

CHaPTer 2

Sara parked in front of the church. Will had been relatively un-obnoxious which wasn't his usual style. She really wished her sister would stop wasting her time on him. Sara was sure she could find another nice young man if she'd look around her every once in a while, instead of always being distracted by Will.

"We should make Sara come with us," Will said, hopping out and getting Sara's wheelchair for her. "She could get us a really good parking spot."

"No, thanks," Sara said as she transferred to her chair. "Malls are boring and full of clothes that are overpriced and will be out of fashion in six months."

"But won't I look fantastic for those six months?" Will mused.

Even Sara couldn't help giggling.

"I'll see you guys inside," he said. "I gotta hit the little boys' room before everything starts."

Sara watched Will march down the hallway. She wanted to shake him. Sara knew exactly why Will kept Abby around and it had nothing to do with being BFFs. She was sure he did like Abby as a person but Abby was too fat for him. Abby wasn't fat—she just wasn't a stick figure. She had a classic figure, like Marilyn Monroe's, but to guys like Will that meant fat. Will kept Abby around because he needed someone who constantly adored him to prop up his own delicate ego. When he got a girlfriend, he dropped Abby faster than a hot potato and she wouldn't see him for weeks. Then she would slump into a grumpy depression until Will broke up with the girlfriend and then it was like the sun was shining again. Abby needed to expand her horizons just a bit bigger than Will's cloud.

They were about to go to their normal bench in the back of the chapel when they noticed someone was sitting there.

"Isn't that the new guy?" Sara whispered to Abby.

Abby nodded, frowning. "Great."

Before Abby could complain too much, Sara rolled forward and parked right next to him in the wheelchair cutout. Abby had no choice but to follow her. The new guy moved over so that Abby could sit down next to her sister.

Sara secretly smiled to herself. Despite what Abby had said back at the house, this new guy didn't look like a weirdo. He looked like a nice guy and if he had been staring at Abby, well, she couldn't blame him. Abby was a beautiful girl—even if Sara's opinion was biased. She had long blonde hair, a perfect, unfreckled complexion that she always highlighted to perfection with an expert makeup job, and always wore classic but fashionable clothes that complimented her hourglass figure. The girl had a talent for sniffing out fashion-forward clothes at second-hand stores like the DI, not to mention Abby's closet full of high heels.

The first few minutes they all sat there awkwardly as the prelude music played. Finally, Sara leaned over.

"Hi, I'm Sara Larsen and this is my sister, Abby," she said. "I've noticed you for the last couple of Sundays. Are you new in the ward?"

"Hi, I'm Brandon Majors," he said, smiling at the sisters. "I just moved here from Seattle for a job."

"Oh, great," Sara said. "How long have you been in the ward?"

"Um, almost a month," Brandon said. "This is the first time anyone but the bishop's said anything to me."

Sara immediately felt a little guilty. There was no excuse for someone to be overlooked in a ward for so long.

"I'm sorry, I guess we should have said something sooner," Sara said. "Welcome to the ward!"

"Thanks!" Brandon said, chuckling and looking over at Abby. Oh, yeah. He had it bad for Abby. "I wasn't sure what to think. It wasn't like this in Seattle. And I wasn't going to a singles' ward there. I didn't even know what a singles' ward was until the bishop in the family ward told me about it. I'm still trying to learn everything. I've only been a member for about a year."

"You're a convert?" Abby asked.

He nodded.

"So were our parents," she said, a little excitement in her voice. "We are sorry we didn't say something earlier. It can be a little confusing coming from a 'mission field' ward. That's what they call wards that aren't in Utah. You can get lost here because of the sheer numbers alone."

"I've noticed," he said, a crooked smile on his face.

"Don't be surprised if it happens a lot, unfortunately," Sara said. "Everyone just assumes if you're in church, you should just know what you're doing or what everyone is talking about. My dad used to say it was like everyone was speaking a foreign language. He had to learn most of it from context."

Brandon laughed at that. "That is definitely true."

"Well, you're welcome to sit with us as long as you want to," Sara said. "We're here most Sundays."

Brandon was about to say something when the bishop got up to the podium and announced the opening prayer. After the prayer, he got up again.

"Thank you, Brother White, for that succinct prayer," Bishop Gold said. He shuffled some papers at the stand. "I'd like to get through these announcements before we start the sacrament. I'd like to announce a few engagements that happened over the week. Let's congratulate Finley Green and Charlie Morgan, Harley Barrett and Gabe Dixon,

Skye Edwards and Tom Dorsey, and then finally Maisie Adams and Neil Merrill on their upcoming weddings."

Abby giggled and leaned over to Sara. "I didn't know Neil was even dating anyone."

"I didn't either," Sara said. "Wasn't Maisie that new girl from two weeks ago?"

"Now that you mention it, I think so."

"That was quick. I can just hear 'Some Enchanted Evening' in my head now."

"Yeah, like that would really happen. They must have known each other from before."

Sara shrugged at her sister.

The foyer doors opened. Sara looked back to see Will peek his head in. Abby noticed him too and nodded towards their pew.

Abby leaned a little over Brandon once Will sat down. "Did you fall in?" she asked teasingly.

"Maybe," he said, giving her a cheeky smile.

"You guys, the prayer," Sara hissed.

After the sacrament prayer, they sat in silence while the men of the ward did their duty. Sara watched Abby and Will snickering to each other as they typed out text messages on their phones. That was another thing Sara didn't like about Will–his penchant for being disrespectful and dragging Abby along with him.

Once that part of the service was over, Abby leaned into Brandon to say something to Will when Brandon said, "Did you guys want to sit together?"

"Sorry, are we being too loud?"

He chuckled. "No, I just think it's funny that you're one person away from each other and you're trying to talk over me. Trade me seats."

"Are you sure?" Abby asked.

"Positive."

He stood up slightly and stepped over her knees so she could scoot under him to sit next to Will. Once he was settled, she said, "Thank you."

Abby and Will chatted quietly to each other through the rest of the sacrament meeting. Brandon looked a little disappointed if Sara could read his face correctly.

After the closing prayer, Abby seemed to realize Brandon was still next to her. She turned to him.

"Do you want to come with us to Sunday School?"

"Thank you, but I believe the bishop said he wanted to see me after," Brandon responded. He did look truly disappointed.

"Well, if you get out in time, find us. We'll save you a seat," Abby said. He looked a lot happier after that.

"He seemed really nice," Sara said as she pushed her wheelchair out to the foyer.

"I'd say so," Abby said.

"Of course she would," Will said. "He couldn't stop staring at her the whole time."

Abby blushed. "Now you're making up stories. He was not."

Will scoffed.

"Are you jealous?" Sara asked, eyeing Will.

"What?" Will said. "No."

Sara laughed. "Sure, cause only *you* noticed."

"Yeah, Will, you did notice, which means you had to have watched him yourself," Abby said, bumping her shoulder into his.

"Can't help it if every time I looked in his direction, he was looking at you like a filet mignon."

"Will, that's not funny to tease about. Maybe he was looking at you and has a crush on you."

"That's too bad for him then," Will said. "All the girls in the ward adore me."

"Except me," Sara said.

"That's just because you're weird and I've known you two forever."

Abby grimaced. Seemed like every time she tried to get even a little flirty with Will, he'd bring up how long Abby had known him. Yet another reason Abby needed to find someone new—someone who didn't think of her as old-hat.

They found seats in the Sunday School room.

"Hi, Will. Oh, hi, Abby." A beautiful girl with long, dark brown hair flounced down next to Will just about sitting on his lap. Olivia Farris had gone to school with Will and Abby and Abby couldn't stand her. Sara's opinion of Olivia was that she was a typical spoiled rich girl who was used to getting everything she wanted. Abby looked like she wanted to strangle her.

"Did you hear?" Olivia asked, resting her arm on Will's shoulder. "Cameron got accepted to Duke University so he's leaving in a couple of weeks to start football camp. I'm going to be so bored. We agreed that we're taking a break for a while. Duke is such a long way away. Anyway, my friends and I want to go to a club to celebrate my freedom. Want to come?"

"Sounds like fun," Will said.

"You could come too, Abby, if you want," Olivia said, giving Abby a glance.

"Oh, gee, thanks so much for thinking of me," Abby said. "I'll think about it."

Good girl, Sara thought. She was afraid Abby was going to say yes purely because Will did. She could only imagine the disaster a setup like that would be for Abby. Have to watch a half-dozen rail-thin girls dancing all over Will while Abby was left off to the side.

They didn't see Brandon for the rest of church, and Sara was only too glad to drop Will back off at his house afterward. He usually insisted on coming over to hang out, but Sara wasn't in the mood for him today. Not after she'd seen how Brandon had looked at her sister. She needed to come up with a way she could encourage Brandon and gently push Abby in his direction and away from Will. Even if nothing came of it, at the very least, maybe going out with Brandon would open Abby's eyes to the fact there were other guys out there who were willing to put her first and treat her the way she deserved to be treated.

CHAPTER 3

The next Sunday, Abby and Will were pushing each other as they walked into the foyer of the church. Will had been playful, pulling Abby's hair and then giving her a big shove each time they approached a door so he could hold it open for her. Sara was apparently not amused.

"You guys are like third graders," Sara said. "First, Will makes us late and then you two are goofing off and—"

They had just sat down in their normal pew when Sara's voice stopped. Abby looked over to see what the matter was with Sara. Sara looked flushed—like she'd seen a ghost. She followed her line of sight to a pew several rows ahead where Olivia sat with a guy Abby had never seen. It had to be a brother or something because he had the same dark hair and light-skinned complexion Olivia did, but he wore glasses.

Will leaned over. "Is Sara okay?" he whispered.

"I think so," Abby said, whispering back. She wondered if Sara knew the guy Olivia was sitting with. "Does Olivia have a brother?"

"I think she does," Will said. "An older brother but I've never met him. He was off to college by the time we moved here."

"I wonder if Sara knows him," Abby said. She was about to ask her sister when she noticed Brandon's head pop through the doorway. The sacrament music was starting. Abby waved him over. He hurried to sit down on their bench right next to Abby.

After the sacrament was over, Abby's phone buzzed. Will bumped her shoulder.

So inviting him to sit with us now, huh?

Why, you jealous? I knew it

**You're delusional
you like him, admit it**

he's new to Salt Lake and he's a convert

**That's what you say now
He's still staring at you**

Good for him

Want me to see if he likes you?

*Don't you dare
I'll put green hair dye in your shampoo
you know I will
your mom will let me in the house*

You're no fun

Guess not

Abby gave Will eye daggers and sat back in her seat. She was not going to let him goad her. And as playful as he'd been today, she wouldn't put it past him to pull something like that. He tried sending her another couple of texts but she wouldn't look at them. He had to know she was serious. Abby folded her arms. She took short glances at Brandon every once in a while during the meeting. She wanted to see what Sara and Will had been teasing her about.

She had to admit that he wasn't a bad-looking guy. He wore a nicely fitted suit complete with a pressed tie with a tie pin, plus a suit coat—most guys in the ward just wore a button-up oxford with whatever tie they pulled out of the closet. He had a stocky frame but he wasn't fat, per se. He had a nicely groomed full beard framing a generous mouth. He glanced at her and gave her a shy smile. She smiled back looking away after noting his kind, blue eyes. So he was good looking and dressed well. Those were bonuses in his favor. The only big negative was that he wasn't more like Will.

After the meeting ended, she and Will walked out of the chapel. Brandon came to stand next to her.

"Ready for Sunday School this time?" she asked him.

"Yes, lead on," he said. She was about to when she heard a voice over the crowd say, "Abby, Will, Sara!"

Abby looked over. Olivia Farris waved at them. "Come meet my brother, Evan."

Abby sized him up pretty quickly now that she had a direct view of him. Evan Farris was fairly average looking, with short brown hair and brown eyes, with a shadow of scruff on his chin and upper lip. Not necessarily attractive to Abby. She looked over at her sister. Sara looked like she'd been hit over the head with a stick.

"Hi," Evan said, reaching out and shaking Will and Abby's hands. His smile got a little bigger when he saw Sara. "Why do you look familiar to me?"

"We went to high school together for a year," Sara said, pink spreading across her cheeks. "I think you were a senior when I was a sophomore."

"Oh, right!" Evan said. "I remember you from the last Christmas concert I did there. You were in the orchestra. Your violin solo was amazing."

"I can't believe you remember that," Sara said, her cheeks blazing an even darker pink.

"Do you still play?"

"I do. I play with the university orchestra. I'm almost done with a double major in art and music."

"That's great," he said, smiling at her. "I hope I get to hear you play at church while I'm here for the summer."

Abby almost laughed out loud. She could only imagine her introverted sister getting up in front of the entire ward to play by herself.

"I'm not great at solos," Sara said.

"If you have a particular piece in mind, I could play the piano accompaniment for you."

"Yeah, Sara, we could invite him over to the Bartons' and use their piano. I bet Crystal would love listening to you two play together."

"Sure, let me give you my number. If you ever want to get together, just let me know."

While Evan gave Sara his phone number, she looked up at Brandon.

"Hey, um, Olivia, Evan, this is Brandon," Abby said smiling, feeling a little dumb to have almost forgotten him even though he was standing right there. "He just moved here from Seattle."

Evan warmly shook his hand in welcome. Olivia gave him a small smile. She was too busy talking with Will. Probably about going out to that club this past week.

"Should we go to class?" Abby said, trying her hardest not to give Olivia eye daggers.

Abby followed behind Olivia and Will, watching them talk. She tried really hard not to get irritated. It's not like Will was her boyfriend. He could talk to whomever he wanted to. Why did it have to be Olivia? Miss I-can't-seem-to-keep-a-boyfriend-longer-than-three-months. She knew why. Olivia was a spoiled brat. She demanded rather than asked, and it was her way or the highway. She was beautiful. Her long brown hair flowed effortlessly into beachy waves and she always had the latest style and perfect makeup. Not to mention she was at best a size three. But most guys didn't like her imperious attitude. She felt bad for the guy Olivia would end up marrying.

"Did you hear what the mid-week activity was this week?" Brandon asked, startling her out of her thoughts.

"Sorry, no, I wasn't paying attention. I don't go to many because I usually have a lot of homework," she said, giving him a slight smile.

"What are you in school for?"

"I'm going to be a pharmacist."

"That is actually the first time I've heard anyone say that but that is really cool."

"It's also a lot of years in school and a lot of information to know off the top of your head."

"I bet. All those drugs to know about and what they do."

"But I could get a job anywhere I wanted if I didn't stay in Utah."

"So you don't plan on staying in Utah forever?"

Abby shrugged her shoulders. "I'm not trying to leave, but if it happens, I won't mind."

"I didn't necessarily want to leave Seattle either, but it was a good job offer and a fresh start."

Abby smiled at him and nodded as she couldn't think of what else to say. They filed into the Relief Society room and, as expected, Will sat next to Olivia which meant that Brandon took the opportunity to sit by Abby. She sighed inwardly.

Abby looked over towards the end of the row. Instead of trying to sit by his sister, Evan was sitting by Sara. Abby couldn't help the small smile that ticked up at the corner of her mouth. They were probably talking about music. Anyone could engage Sara in an immediate conversation if they brought up the topic. And Evan certainly won bonus points with her sister if he could play the piano. But he won points with Abby because he seemed genuinely interested in Sara. She wondered if this interest on Sunday might translate into being interested during the week too. She hoped so.

She looked up and saw Brandon watching her.

"Do you know Evan very well?" Brandon asked.

"I don't," Abby said. "Olivia, his sister, and I were in the same grade in high school. I only knew her, but it seems my sister knew Evan a little."

"He seems attentive," Brandon said, smiling as he shot a glance at the pair.

"You think so?" Abby said. "Most guys are just polite to her."

Brandon shook his head. "I know guys and that's not a 'polite' nice."

#Abby smiled at Brandon. "You certainly seem to think you know a lot."

"I know a few things," he said.

"Like what?" she asked.

"Like I'm pretty sure you'd trade places with Olivia if you could," he said, raising his eyebrows at Will.

She looked over at the pair still talking. "Because of Will? Oh, he and I have been friends forever."

Brandon didn't look convinced.

"What makes you so certain of yourself?"

"Because you've been peeking glances at him when you're not keeping an eye on your sister," he said.

Abby grimaced. "Even if you were sort of right, which you're not, he doesn't look at me like that. He never has."

"His loss, in my opinion."

"And you seem to have quite a few of those," Abby said. It was hard to keep herself from blushing at his implied compliment. In reality, even if she did like him a little, he was much too old for her. He looked to be in his middle to late twenties. She was nineteen.

He shrugged. "I suppose so."

The class started, effectively cutting off further discussion, but she couldn't help thinking about what he'd said. It bothered her. Was she that obvious about Will? No one but Sara knew how much she really liked him, or at least she'd thought so. But if Brandon, whom she hadn't met until last week could see right through her, it made her wonder if Will could, too. If he could, would he still want to hang out with her? Probably not. Not that she didn't wish he would have deeper feelings for her. It was hard to watch him flirt it up with girls like Olivia. Her only comfort was in knowing that when he wasn't dating them, he was hanging out with her. But that wasn't quite the same as him having romantic feelings for her.

She glanced over at Evan and Sara. They weren't talking anymore but she thought she could sense a comfortableness about them. Maybe it was just her wishful thinking for her sister, but it was almost as if they should be sitting shoulder to shoulder or holding hands or something. They weren't but it looked like they could. She leaned back in her chair and tried to pay attention to the lesson.

The girl teaching the lesson asked a question about some aspect of missionary work.

Brandon raised his hand.

"I'm a recent convert," he said. "Religion wasn't something I'd ever contemplated in my whole life, but after my divorce, I felt like I needed something different in my life. Like my life up to then had been missing something. That also meant I wanted more for my son. Right around that time, a friend of mine shared a miraculous experience he'd had praying for a family member, and that's how we got to talking about the Church and his beliefs. And I realized that's what I'd been missing. He got me connected with the missionaries and, well, for me the rest was history. But if my friend had been afraid to talk about the gospel, or if he'd kept how he felt about his faith to himself, I would still be wandering around wondering what I was missing. Instead, I'm here, sure of my faith and sure of the knowledge that I'm a son of God."

Abby watched him as he talked. Listening to him tell his story sounded so much like her parents. They'd had a similar story. They'd wanted something more but they didn't know where to find it, so they sort of church bounced until they ran into some missionaries at a park one day. They got to talking to these two young men and then it was like a lightbulb had been turned on and they could finally see everything clearly for the first time. It was also where Abby and Sara had gotten their terrible names—Abish and Sariah. Their dad in particular had a love of the Book of Mormon. Her dad used to always gently chastise them about the fact that though their names were unusual to the world, they were two examples of women of faith who overcame such great trials that they deserved mention in the Book of Mormon where the high respect placed on women meant they were rarely mentioned.

Her parents had always been fantastic examples of faithfulness. Her dad may have fit the profile of a fanatic more than their mother but that also had its benefits—he read everything he could, so if they ever had questions about anything, they knew who to ask.

That was one thing she missed most about her dad—being able to go ask him questions when she wasn't sure what to think. Like what to do about Will, or even this guy Brandon. Or about her future as a young woman, a future wife and mother, and career woman.

With Sunday School over she got up and waited for the rest of the row to leave. She looked at Brandon's back. She felt a different level of respect for him and on impulse she tapped him on the shoulder. He turned to look at her.

"Do you have plans for dinner tonight?" she asked.

"No, unless you count a ham sandwich, a Coke, and a recording of the latest Seattle Seahawks game," he said, smiling.

"Sara is a whiz with the crockpot and I'm sure we have room for one more if you'd like to join us," Abby said.

"I would, thanks," he said.

Abby handed her phone to him. "Let me have your number and I'll text you the directions to our house."

She wondered briefly if she was making a mistake by encouraging him. She didn't want him to think there was more going on with her than there was. Yet, it wasn't her responsibility to look out for his feelings when all she was trying to do was start a friendship. For her part, based on her parents' experiences, she knew new converts didn't have it easy in this area and being one could be lonely if you didn't have family.

CHAPTER 4

On the way home, Abby told Sara what she'd done.

"That's a good idea," Sara said. "I should text Evan and see if he wants to as well."

"I love that you got Evan's number so quickly," Abby said, giggling.

Sara started to blush. "Well, we're going to do a violin and piano duet in a few weeks."

Abby's smile got bigger. "And I'm just as shocked that he got you to agree to that as well. Did I miss the part where he threatened your life?"

"No," Sara's blush deepened. "He just asked and I said yes."

Her wide grin continued to grow until it was positively Cheshire. "You like him."

"Yes, I do like him."

"I mean, "like" like him. Like really like him."

Sara glanced over at her sister. "I've . . . I've always liked him. Since high school. I just figured after he graduated from high school, I'd never see him again. And well, to be honest, I didn't think he'd ever notice me. I didn't think he ever had."

"He sure noticed you today," Abby said.

"I guess," Sara said, turning into the driveway of their house. "We had a nice time talking. Do you think I should make rolls to go with dinner? Maybe you could make some dessert—make it a real dinner for once?"

Abby nodded, the Cheshire grin still on her face. "I can do that. I'm also texting Will. He'll want to come too."

"Do you have to?" Sara asked.

"Why not Will?" Abby asked.

"I just thought you were inviting Brandon over to get to know him better," Sara said, getting out of the car.

"I am. So we can all get to know him better," Abby said, following her sister into the house. "He's a new convert just like Mom and Dad were. I'm sure he's spent a lot of time on his own since he moved here. Did you hear that he has a little boy? Well, it sounds like his little boy spends most of his time with his mother, so if I were him, I'd be lonely."

"That's true," Sara said, giving Abby her own smile. "As long as Will doesn't try to dominate the conversation."

"Will's just naturally boisterous," Abby said.

"You mean naturally an attention hog, and rude?" Sara said.

Abby rolled her eyes. "Whatever. He is what he is. I thought you liked him."

"I like Will in small doses. He's not a bad guy. He's just good-looking and he knows it. Too much."

"You can't know you're good-looking too much."

Sara shook her head as she went into the kitchen.

"Well, I think it's good you invited Brandon over," Sara said. "It'll be good for him to have friends now that he's on his own."

Abby pulled out the dishes that once belonged to her mom. Her mom would have loved doing something like this. She was one of those women that took people under her wing, and food was one of the ways she spoiled them with love. Her apples didn't fall far from her tree, it seemed.

Abby went to the hallway bathroom to give it a once-over since they were having company. She looked in the mirror and frowned. She pulled at her cheeks and under her chin. She hated her round face. Definitely not thin enough to get Will's attention when Olivia was around. Definitely not thin enough to get most of the men in the ward's attention when most of the girls there seemed to be a size nine or lower. Well, except maybe Brandon's.

He seemed like a nice guy, maybe a little over-opinionated, but still nice. What if Brandon did ask her out? She wasn't sure. He was a little too old for her, and he'd already been married and had a kid. How would she deal with being an insta-mommy when she was years away from finishing her degree and starting her career.

Not that any of that mattered right now. She was getting ahead of herself. Brandon hadn't asked her out. They'd barely known each other for a couple of weeks. Maybe he never planned to. Maybe he was too shy or maybe when he got to know her a bit better, he would decide he didn't like her. He could be like any other male in the ward who expected a girl to look like Ariana Grande or Taylor Swift when he looked like Barney Rubble. Then all this worrying about him asking her out would be for nothing and more like fluffing her own ego.

A while later, the doorbell rang and she went to answer it. Brandon stood at the door with a plate in his hands.

"Hi, what's this?" Abby asked.

"My world-famous Monster Cookies," he said, holding the plate up for her to take. "I hope no one has a peanut allergy."

"Sara and I don't," Abby said, taking it from him and letting him in the house. She was pleased to note that his dressing well extended to his down time. He wore a nice-fitting t-shirt with a pair of dark denim jeans. They actually accentuated his stout figure rather than making him look dumpy. "These smell awesome. What's in them?"

"Peanut butter, oatmeal, a little bit of flour, chocolate chips and chocolate candy pieces, and, because I'm extra fancy, toffee bits."

"Oh, those do sound good," Sara said, coming out from the kitchen covered in flour. "I'll put them in the fridge for later."

"What happened to you?"

"My world-famous dinner rolls to go with our dinner of crockpot stroganoff," she said, taking the plate.

"Sounds like I picked a good night to get invited to dinner," Brandon said, a big smile on his face. He took a seat on the couch in the front room."

"And, because I'll take any chance to brag about my sister—" Abby said, sitting down on the loveseat across from him, "any night is a good night when she makes dinner. I'm an okay cook, but she is the best."

"Good to know," he said.

"So, Brandon," Sara said, coming into the room and wiping off her clothes with a kitchen rag. "You have a little boy?"

"Yes, his name is Colin," Brandon said. "He's four, almost five. His birthday's this spring."

"Colin. I like that name," Abby said, smiling.

"Want to see him?"

"Yes!"

Brandon pulled out his phone and scrolled through a few pictures. He gave her the phone and she and Sara looked at the picture of a small boy around the age of three. He was blonde with blue eyes just like his dad's, and had his dad's same smile. He held tightly to a red balloon and had dirt smudges all over his jean overalls.

"Oh, he's so cute," Sara said. "He looks a little like you."

"He takes mostly after my ex-wife Michelle's side of the family, but there's a little of me in there too."

"I bet you miss him," Abby said.

"I do," he said, the smile turning sad. "Eight hundred miles is a big distance, especially since I was used to seeing him everyday."

Abby couldn't imagine, though she wanted to be sympathetic. She and Sara had never spent any significant time apart and she knew that the years were quickly coming where they would have to, but if it felt the same as being apart from her sister, then it would be bad enough.

"You said in class that your friend introduced you to the missionaries. Can we hear your conversion story?" Sara asked. "I know it sounds cheesy to ask but we love hearing them."

"A buddy of mine at work, Alex, was helping me while I was going through my divorce. He'd been through one himself, and he was there to listen when I needed it. We got to talking about spiritual help, like prayer and getting personal answers, one day. I swear we stayed up all night just talking because I had all these questions. He got me in contact with the missionaries and, well, after that it was sort of a whirlwind because I couldn't find out things fast enough. I mean my parents are great people but they were never really spiritual and didn't raise me that way. They just taught me to be a good person and that was enough. I think they're still scratching their heads wondering why I joined a church, let alone the Mormon church."

"Why did you join?" Abby asked.

"Because everything I was hearing was making sense," he said. She saw the familiar conviction, like her father's, in his eyes. "Even the stuff that might have sounded farfetched at first. The more I read, the more it made sense. And when I would pray about it, this feeling would come over me and I couldn't deny that was something that'd never happened to me before. It was like He knew me personally and was encouraging me to know as much as I could. So when the missionaries asked me if I wanted to be baptized, I didn't really have to think about it too hard."

"That's so amazing," Sara said, smiling. "I love hearing stories like that. We told you our parents were converts. And it's so strange considering my mom comes from one of the oldest families that originally settled Riverton, so there must have been members of the Church at some point. They just fell away, I guess. Our parents were two crazy hippy types. They liked wandering around to different places across the country and didn't stay in any place too long. But one day they were in Philadelphia, I think, and they came across some missionaries teaching at a park and they started talking to them. And it was kind of like what you said—they just had so many questions. I think it was because my mom had found out she was pregnant with me at the time and now it wasn't just about her and Dad. My dad, though, he read everything! He was like a church encyclopedia. You could ask him anything and if he'd read about it he'd be able to tell you everything about it. He was awesome."

"Was?" Brandon asked gently.

"Oh, yeah, he died of prostate cancer about five years ago," Sara said, deflated a little.

"I'm sorry," Brandon said.

"We are, too," Sara said. "And Mom died of breast cancer a couple of years after that. Total fluke. So it's just Abby and me now."

"Man, that's a lot in a short amount of time," he said.

"Like Sara said, we have a lot of family around," Abby said. "This is our mother's cousin's house. She lets us *rent* it from her for a really low amount, basically enough to cover most of the taxes every year and then we pay the utilities. They've been a huge support."

"That is amazing to have a family like that," Brandon said. "I'm glad you both have that support nearby."

"Our parents are also why we have a soft spot for new converts," Abby said, though she tried to cover her grimace. "It hasn't been easy. After their baptism they decided they'd move to Utah because they thought of it as some sort of Mormon Mecca, and they'd be welcomed open-armed by the members here and everything would be hunky-dory. But it never was. They were a little too weird, a little too hippy to really fit in and that's why my dad was so determined to find out everything for himself. No one ever stepped forward to mentor either of them to make sure they understood how everything works. They had to figure everything out themselves so they used to joke that they would take in the strays of the ward whenever they could."

"Am I a stray?" Brandon said with a half grin on his face.

"Yes," Abby said. "You've landed right in the middle of the boiling pot of Utah Mormon culture. I'm sure you've already figured out how confusing that can be. We just wanted to make sure you knew you have friends who understand and want to help."

"Oh, I see how it is," he said. leaning towards her. "I thought it was my irresistible personality and devastating good looks." He gave her a big toothy grin.

Abby stood up off the couch when another knock came at the door. "You might be getting a little ahead of yourself there, Brandon."

She could have sworn she heard him mumble, "A man's gotta dream."

Will stood at the door playing with his phone. "I invited Olivia since Evan was coming, is that okay?"

Abby grimaced. "No, it isn't. You should have called first."

"Sorry," he said, though he didn't look sorry in the least.

Abby looked over at Sara. Sara rolled her eyes and shrugged. "Guess I'm getting out another place setting," Sara said.

Abby snatched Will's phone out of his hand. "Seriously, Will. That wasn't cool. You didn't even ask."

Will looked at her with his big blue eyes. "Sorry. I didn't think it would be that big of a deal. Evan was already coming."

"Yeah, but just because Evan was invited doesn't mean Olivia was." She could smack him. She closed the door a bit harder than she intended to and the picture of her parents on the wall next to the door shook.

"Okay, okay," Will said loudly, pouting, snatching his phone back from Abby. "I won't do it again. Sheesh."

Abby went and sat down on the couch next to Brandon.

"I could kick him out for you, if you'd like," he said, leaning over so only she could hear it.

She couldn't help giving him a small smile. "No. He'd only stand outside and whine that we'd left him out in the cold. I'll make sure to make his life sufficiently miserable later."

Brandon gave her an encouraging smile.

"So, Will, do you work or go to school?" Brandon asked as Will continued to play on his phone.

"I work," he said. "At a call center. I hate it but it pays the bills."

"Are you planning to go to school later?"

"No. I'm not sure what I'm going to do," he said.

"Okay," Brandon said. "Good plan."

Will finally picked up on the sarcasm in Brandon's voice. "What do you do?"

"I'm a software engineer at Adobe," he said. "I'm on a team of about ten people and I hope to be in management in the next five years."

"How old are you?"

"Twenty-five."

"Nice. I guess you do that kind of stuff when you get old. Manage people and stuff."

"Yup, you kind of do, when you get old," Brandon said. His face remained neutral. Abby held up a hand to her face, wanting to laugh. Brandon looked over at Abby and winked.

"What?" Will asked.

The doorbell rang and Sara answered it this time. Evan and Olivia stood there. Evan held a bottle of soda in his hand and Olivia held a pie of some sort.

"Welcome," Sara said, giving Evan a huge smile.

"I thought since we were invited last minute, we'd bring something along," Evan said, holding up the bottle. As soon as Olivia walked through the door, Will hurried over to offer his help.

Abby wanted to gag or hit Will over the head. Preferably both. As if she couldn't carry a pie by herself. Abby got up off the couch and was pleased to note that Evan immediately made himself useful in the kitchen with Sara. He carried the crockpot to the table and took the basket of rolls from her as well.

"These smell wonderful," he said, giving Sara a warm smile.

"It's her specialty," Abby confirmed. "They'll melt in your mouth."

"Then I can't wait to try one," he said. Sara couldn't look more pleased and more flushed if she'd tried.

Abby retrieved their salad and went to sit down. Brandon was right there pulling the chair out for her. "Thanks," she said.

"Always," he said. "My momma didn't raise a slob."

The rest of dinner went well without further drama, though it was hard to concentrate on what anyone else was saying with Olivia and Will being so loud.

Every once in a while, Abby would peek over at how Evan and Sara were doing. They seemed to not notice anything going on with Will and Olivia, and were just off in their own little world. She really hoped for her sister's sake that Evan was the start of good things for her. The only thing that worried her was that Evan was only there for the summer. She'd hate for Sara to get attached to him, only to have him move back to Arizona in August—or who knows where else in the country after that. She wondered what he planned on majoring in. He didn't seem like the type that'd go for something like politician or lawyer. More like a scruffy professor who wore tweed suit jackets with leather patches on the elbows and pipe in his mouth. The thought made her giggle in spite of herself.

"What's got you giggling over there?" Brandon asked.

"Oh, just contemplating something silly," she said. "I see my sister and Evan talking and I just have hope for her."

"You mean because of the wheelchair thing?" he asked.

"Yes," Abby said. "You can't deny that it deters most guys."

"I guess it might," he said. "I just think Evan sees her as an interesting person. Kind of like I see you."

Abby gave him a look. "I was talking about my sister. As much as I think Evan would be perfect for her, he's from a rich family. I've been listening to Olivia talk about him. Apparently, they have some sort of expectation for him to live up to. Would that include someone like my sister? Would she be good enough for him in their eyes? Some orphaned girl in a wheelchair with no money and doesn't know anyone important enough for them? It's not like us being related to the oldest family in Riverton really means anything to anyone except those families in Riverton."

"I guess the question should be how much should it matter to someone like Evan? Would he worry about what his family thinks, or would he follow his heart?"

Abby looked at Brandon. "I don't know. I don't know him at all. He seems like a nice enough guy, but when it comes to family, you just never know."

Loud laughter erupted from the other end of the table where Will and Olivia sat. Abby looked over at them, and sighed in frustration. Why did he have to invite Olivia? Not that Brandon was terrible to talk to but she'd invited Will over so she could talk to him too. Now she was practically invisible, with Olivia here.

"That's true," Brandon said, "But there's also something to be said for someone knowing what they want when it comes to love."

"I'm sure you know all about that, having been married before," she said. She wasn't accusing him necessarily, but she also wanted to remind him that his first marriage wasn't exactly the most successful.

"It's just as true with my first marriage as it is for anything else," he said. "You think you know what you want, and you go for it. Then you find out that what you thought you wanted wasn't what you really wanted, or that the person you thought you wanted didn't have what you thought they did. Then you find yourself splitting up. In my case, I didn't necessarily want to get divorced. I cared for Michelle. Still do. But we agreed that both of us would be happier, and Colin would be happier, with us separate."

"I guess that's the best you can expect in a situation like that," Abby said. "So many people who get divorced seem like they hate each other."

"It's a conscious decision both people have to agree to," Brandon said. "Michelle and I might have looked like we didn't like each other very much during the process. Ultimately we agreed that our son's happiness was what we both wanted most, so anything else didn't matter. She's free to live her life the way she wants. I'm doing the same, and we try to co-parent the best we can."

"How does she feel about you joining the Church?" Abby asked.

"I'm still not sure she knows what to make of it," Brandon said. "But she's agreed to let me take him to church with me and do church things if he wants, but she's asked me to let him decide if he wants to and then wait until he's eighteen if he wants to join too. I felt that was fair."

"She seems like a decent person, even if you couldn't stay married," Abby said.

"She is," Brandon said. "But enough about her. What about you?"

"What about me?"

"Besides that you're becoming a pharmacist, I don't know very much about you."

"Well, I like virgin pina coladas, and walking in the rain," she smiled at him. "Just kidding. I'm probably pretty boring compared to people you know. You know, old people. But I like shopping at second-hand stores and finding designer labels in my style. I love shoes, especially high heels. I have an embarrassingly large number of shoes in my collection. And I like to be outdoors when I don't have tons of homework to do."

"Shoes, huh?" he said.

Abby blushed a little. "Just a few."

She looked around. It looked like everyone was done with their dinner.

"Evan and Olivia brought pie and Brandon brought cookies. I'll leave them out for anyone that's interested."

She walked over to the kitchen and got out a pie server.

Brandon walked up behind her. "What would you say if I asked you out?" he asked.

She opened her mouth to say something. She glanced over at the table. Will sat there staring at the both of them. There was something in his look that suddenly made Abby angry. There was a possessiveness about it. She narrowed her eyes at him and looked away.

She turned to look at Brandon. "Sure. I have school most days but I'm done by late afternoon. I'm free most evenings. Wednesdays are usually when the ward has their weekly activities. So pretty much any other day."

"Great!" he said with a big smile on his face. "How about tomorrow?"

Her lips curled up in a half-smile. "In a big hurry?"

"No, but I figure why wait? What do you like to do?"

"Riverton has a really nice old park not too far from here. How about we just walk around and talk? Meet me at the baseball diamonds off of 1300 West."

"Six p.m.? Then maybe dinner?"

"Sure."

After everyone had left, Sara rolled over to the couch where Abby sat, and transferred over. Laying her head on her sister's lap, she sighed.

"I like him, Abby," she said.

"I know," Abby said. "Did he ask you out?"

"No," Sara said. "He wants to get together to practice the violin solo a couple of times this week. Does that count?"

"Sort of . . ." Abby said. "Where at? The church?"

"We don't have the keys. I was thinking of calling Crystal and seeing if we could borrow her piano."

"Are you sure you want to do that?" Abby said, looking down at her sister. "You know she thinks she's got the right to take the place of Mom and she'll be all over Evan."

"I think Evan will take it in good grace," Sara said.

"Let's hope so," Abby said, chuckling. "Poor guy."

"What about you? Did Brandon ask you out?"

"Yes, for tomorrow."

"Really? That fast, huh?"

"He said he didn't see a need to wait. I don't mind really. He's really nice. The only problem is, Sara, isn't he a little too old for me? He's twenty-five."

"Maybe, but give him a chance; see how much you both have in common first. If there's nothing there, then there's nothing there. Nothing says you are required to date him just because he asked you."

#"Will you hate me if I admit something?"

"Probably not."

"I may have said yes because I was mad at Will."

Sara giggled. "Oh, Abby. That's like the worst reason to say yes to another guy."

"I know!" Abby said, burying her face in a pillow. "I just was getting so angry watching him flirt it up with Olivia. In *my* house, no less. And he invited her to dinner without even asking us. What is up with that? Since when does he think he can do that?"

"Since you spoil him rotten with attention any other time so he thinks he can get away with it."

"Yeah, well, things are about to change. I'm not letting him do that again. And if he really wants to be my friend, or anything more than that, he's going to have to put in a little more effort."

"Good! Finally! I'm so proud of you. I should give Brandon a big old kiss and hug."

Abby scoffed. "It's not because of him."

Sara laughed. "Yeah, right."

Chapter 5

Sara smoothed down her blouse and ran her fingers through her hair before she rang the doorbell. Evan's house was in one of the new developments in Riverton along the Jordan River, and the house was enormous. It looked like a Parade of Homes leftover and suddenly Sara felt extremely nervous. She'd always known Evan and Olivia's parents were wealthy—Olivia never left alone a chance to remind people of the fact—but it was one thing to hear it and quite another to see it displayed so obviously.

The woman who answered the door looked like Olivia. She had the same sleek brown hair, severe but beautiful dark eyes and facial features. Evan must look more like his father. His face was softer and kinder.

"Can I help you?" she said coldly.

"I'm here to pick up Evan," Sara said. "I'm Sara Larsen. We're in the same singles ward."

His mother acknowledged her but her eyes scanned Sara from the top of her head down to the bottom of her wheels. Sara bit the inside of her lip and managed a small smile.

"Mom, is Sara here?" Sara could hear Evan's voice from inside the house. Her heart sped up a little when she heard him say her name.

"She is," she said, turning her head inside. "You didn't tell me she was in a wheelchair."

Sara blinked. What did that matter?

"I didn't think it mattered," he said, as he approached the doorway. "Hi! Ahem, Sara, this is my mom. Sara plays the violin. In fact, in my senior year of high school she played the violin solo at the Christmas concert where I performed my piano solo."

Evan smiled at Sara, obviously proud of her, but his mother looked less than impressed.

"Very nice," she said. "Don't be all day practicing. We have a dinner with the Mathesons tonight."

She walked away without saying goodbye. Sara bit her lip but waved at her disappearing back anyway.

"Sorry about that," Evan said, holding his music folder.

"It's okay," Sara said. "She seems, um . . . cordially distant."

"Is that a nice way of saying *cold*?"

"Maybe."

He laughed.

"So my mother's cousin, Crystal, and her husband have this beautiful baby grand at their house. I've already called to let her know we're on our way. She said to just knock once and come in," Sara said, getting into her car.

"Can I help you?" Evan asked, when he saw her breaking down her wheelchair.

"If you like," Sara said, smiling. "And thank you for asking first."

She instructed him on how to break it down further so it fit in the back of her car and then once he was in, she drove away.

"I have to give you fair warning," Sara said, looking over at him. "Crystal is very kind and very welcoming, but she can be overwhelming to some people. Her husband, Todd, is very quiet. Sort of his yang to her yin."

"So what you're saying is that I'm going to walk through the door and she's going to ask us when we're getting married and how many children we're having?"

Sara laughed out loud and blushed her deepest red. "Yes, exactly."

"I've dealt with people like her before," Evan said. "They mean well. I won't be embarrassed if you won't be."

"I'll try not to be," Sara said. "I do love her very much. She was a huge support after Mom died so soon after Dad and I know she just wants me to have every happiness in the world. But just because you come over with me doesn't mean you're the one destined to give it to me, you know?"

"Well, how do you know that?" Evan asked. "What if I am the guy that's supposed to make you the happiest girl in the world and all I need is that not-so-gentle shove in the right direction?"

Sara covered her hand over her mouth and giggled. "I don't. I just don't want you to get your hopes up too high."

"Oh, so it's not about me. It's you who needs a shove in *my* direction."

"Maybe," she said, though she wasn't sure how her face could get any redder, but the smile he gave her said he didn't seem to think anything of it.

How could Evan make her laugh and blush at the same time? She would like very much to see if he really was the person that would make her the happiest girl in the world. They'd only been barely reacquainted, if reacquainted is what you could call her coming back into his orbit and him discovering her for the first time. But in that short time, she was pretty sure of what she knew about him. He had a lot of the things in a guy that she'd always hoped to have in a husband—he was talented, funny, good-looking, smart, and a faithful church-goer.

Don't get your hopes up, Sara, she told herself. *He had the opportunity to ask you out last Sunday and he didn't take it. He probably just sees you as a good friend. They always do. No matter how flirty or kind or interested they act, you always end up getting friend-zoned. Getting your hopes up just gets them crushed.*

She had to give herself this little pep talk every time, but this time even more so. When they talked at church and then afterwards at her house, the conversation between them had been fun, light-hearted and easy. It was a nice surprise. Usually it took a while for her to feel comfortable enough to have an intelligent conversation with someone. But he'd started talking music right away and it was like he was speaking her language. She felt like she could talk to him about anything. And he seemed genuinely interested in hearing about her plans and dreams. She could have talked to him for hours and not noticed, except for one small thing.

She'd told him all about her plans after college to get work in a museum or pursue her own work as an artist, and teach violin lessons to make a living. He acted really excited about all those ideas for her. But when it came to him and what he planned, he was pretty quiet on the subject. He always managed to turn it back around to her or to change the subject to things a little less specific. It bothered her a little because the most he would say was he'd graduated with an English degree from Arizona State and now was trying to decide what he wanted to do with it for graduate school.

Not that it was that big a deal. If you didn't know, you didn't know. Couldn't fault him for having a lot of options. It was important to her to love her occupation, so, of course, a man, who expected to be the provider for his family, would have to choose wisely. She couldn't imagine being stuck in a job you hated merely because that was the only way you knew how to earn money. Soul-sucking. That was the word she thought of.

What bothered her most was he kept a lot about himself to himself. He didn't really talk about himself, but was intent on listening to her talk. People rarely gave her the chance to warm up enough to get a good conversation going, so she usually listened more than she talked. She truly didn't mind listening. It was nice to have someone besides Abby listen to her for once. But besides what she knew about him from high school, and that he had a bachelor's in English and was contemplating graduate school somewhere for . . . something, she didn't know a whole lot about him.

She pulled up to the house, only half a block down the street from hers.

"Wow, she lives really close to you, doesn't she? I should have come to you."

"She does. Apparently what happened was our house belonged to an elderly sister in my cousin's ward who ended up with dementia, but this was during the recession and her children couldn't get anyone to buy the house. So, Todd and Crystal bought it intending to use it as a rental property. And they did for a while but when my mom died, they decided when Abby turned eighteen, they'd let us use it so we could live independently."

"That's really amazing of them."

"That's only one of the reasons we love them so much. They've done so much for us. But even still, she's just so . . . much."

Evan gave her a sympathetic smile. "It's okay."

She pulled up to her cousin's house. "Ready?"

"As ready as you are," he said.

"Then I guess I'm taking you back home," Sara said, taking in a deep breath.

"Come on," Evan said. "I'm willing to bet she's not that bad. It's just because she's family. Our families always manage to embarrass us even if their hearts are in the right place. As you've already witnessed." He said it with a grimace.

"Okay, you're probably right," Sara said. "Let's go."

Sara knocked on the door and then opened it a little. "Crystal, Evan and I are here."

"Oh, good, you're here!" a boisterous voice called from the house. "Come in. I want to meet this young man you've been telling me about."

A large woman ran into the room and enveloped Sara in a bone-cracking hug. "We need to have you and Abby over for dinner soon. It's been too long."

"We would love to," Sara said, when she could get some oxygen into lungs. "Crystal, this is Evan. He's going to accompany me on the piano in a few Sundays. You and Todd should come that Sunday."

"Oh, Evan, welcome," Crystal said, grabbing Evan and hugging him tightly too. Evan smiled down at Sara. "I can't wait to hear you play. If you're as good on the piano as Sara is on the violin then it will be such a treat. I don't get to play much anymore. I used to be quite good myself."

"We should have you play for us then," Evan said.

"Psh, I'm waiting to hear you two play," she said. "But I won't crowd you. I have a few things to do around the house, so I'll let you guys get in as much practice time as you need. Just let me know before you leave."

After Crystal left the room, Sara pulled out her music stand and set up the sheet music. She handed Evan the accompaniment for the hymn *Come Thou Fount of Every Blessing.*

He stared at it for a moment. "I haven't heard this one in a very long time," he said quietly. "I'm glad you chose it."

"It's a special arrangement my friend from school did for me," she said. "It's such a beautiful melody but the way he interweaved the piano makes it so much more magical."

Evan gave her an A to tune her violin with and when she was ready, they started. She watched him as they played. He worked the keys effortlessly. She was a little jealous. Sight-reading had always been one weakness of hers, but she watched as he quickly picked up the notes and their song blended until it nearly had her in tears, it was so beautiful. She had to turn away to blink away some of the moisture before she looked at him again.

"I'm almost disappointed," Evan said.

"Why?"

"Because you played so beautifully, now there's not much of an excuse to practice as much as I'd hoped," he said. Her heart leapt around her chest a little. He wanted to spend time with her, it seemed, as much as she did him. And if he wanted to spend time with her, maybe he had wanted to ask her out but chickened out, or maybe he'd wanted to wait a bit. There could have been lots of reasons he hadn't.

"Thanks," she said. "You did, too, you know. I've always been a little jealous of people who could sight-read so easily."

He looked at her. "I'm surprised you struggle with any aspect of playing the violin. You make it look so easy."

"No. Definitely a lot of practice involved, and looking more confident than I feel."

"Then you do it very well," he said. "Play again, just so I can hear it again?"

Sara could feel color coming into her cheeks but she smiled at him and nodded. She played again but she had a hard time looking away from Evan. Just like talking to him, she could sit here all day and play with him if it were possible. His ease at the piano made it so easy. His encouragement and admiration of her talent had her heart soaring. She sent up a small prayer that maybe things were going the way she hoped.

"That was just lovely, Sara," Crystal said, coming back into the room. "Such a wonderful hymn. So full of hope and the promise of God's love."

"It definitely sounds better with Evan at the piano," Sara said.

"I agree," Crystal said. "You have a delightful nuance, Evan."

"Thank you," he said. "I really do enjoy playing, so I try to whenever I can. It also helps to have someone as talented as Sara to play with." Sara couldn't entirely hide the smile of pleasure his compliment inspired. She could only try and not let it split her face.

Crystal looked like she was ready to burst with pride. "She has always been so talented, and the fact that she's amazingly beautiful doesn't hurt either." Crystal winked at Sara.

Sara was about to protest when Evan said, "Very true, Crystal. I'm glad she's decided to be my friend."

In less than ten seconds, Evan had sent her to the heights of hope, only to slam her back down to Earth again.

"I'll call you when we have time to rehearse again," Sara said, only managing a partial smile. "And I'll let Abby know you want to have dinner. Just text me when you want us to come over."

"Great. And when you come, make sure you bring Evan," Crystal said with a sly smile on her face.

"I wouldn't mind at all," he said.

Sara bit her lip. She wished Crystal hadn't said anything at all. They got in Sara's car and started the drive back to Evan's house.

She glanced at him and her stomach sank. He looked a little different than he had in high school. He was still well-groomed, but he'd added a bit of facial hair. She liked it. It made him look older and more sophisticated. He still had those kind brown eyes that attracted her in the first place. She couldn't help that her stomach flipped a little and her heart sped up a bit when she looked at him—except now that he'd made it clear he didn't feel the same way, her heart also sank. She looked at him knowing regardless of how much she might like him, he would be like every other guy she had a crush on. Disappointment filled the space where her heart had been.

She was used to disappointment, and used to being passed over. Other people took for granted how easy it was to find a date, or even an eternal companion. It's why getting her degree, finding a job and setting up lessons was so important for her. The Lord might see fit for her to live her life on her own. Others might not be able to see what He saw in her, to see past the wheelchair. In that case, she was determined to live her best life doing the things she loved to do.

Evan turned to Sara after a while. "You've been kind of quiet. Is everything okay?"

"Yes, everything's fine."

"Okay,' he said, not looking totally convinced. "Crystal seems like a very nice woman. I'd be happy to go to dinner at their house with you."

"Great. I'll let you know when she calls me."

Evan watched her. "Sara, I wanted to let you know that I have really liked getting to know you. Makes me wonder why we didn't know each other better in high school. Probably me being a dork and thinking I was the cool senior or something. I think we could have been really great friends. You're fun to hang out with. But things are complicated in my life right now. I think I need to let you know about my time down at Arizona State."

"What about it?"

"I went to school there and was seeing—"

Evan's phone rang. "Yes, I'm on my way back right now. What? Why? Great. Okay, I'll probably be there in five minutes."

Evan hung up and a huge grimace spread across his face. "I'm glad we got at least a little time to hang out today." He sighed.

"Everything okay?" Sara asked. Now she was worried for him.

"Not sure yet," he said. "I'll find out when I get home."

She didn't want to press him but his answer was so cryptic, and he didn't seem inclined to divulge any further information.

"I'll see you on Sunday," he said, leaning down to look at Sara while he reached in to grab his folder out of the car.

"Okay, see you then," she said.

As he walked away, she could swear his shoulders looked a little more slumped than they had.

CHAPTER 6

Sara smoothed her hands down her jeans. Evan hadn't arrived yet. She was seriously tempted to text him and tell him dinner had been cancelled and to just go home. She loved Crystal; she really did. Evan had already gotten a small dose of her the other day. But the winks and the innuendo from that day haunted Sara. Crystal, in her enthusiasm to secure Sara's happiness, might very well have scared it off instead. Evan had taken it in good grace but he'd only been in her presence for five minutes all together. This was going to be an entire evening.

"Is Evan here yet?" Abby said, walking into the room. "You look like you're going to be sick."

"I might be," Sara admitted.

"I'll help deflect her. Evan will be fine. He seems like a laid-back guy. He'll probably just laugh about it later," Abby said.

"I hope so," Sara said. "I just don't want Crystal scaring him off. 'Wow, I really dodged a bullet with that family. They're crazy.'"

"Everyone has crazy family members, sis," Abby said. "Some are just more . . . obvious than others."

Someone knocked on the door. Sara's heart leapt and she hurried to answer it. Evan stood there, looking good in a simple polo and jeans. He could be wearing a seventies ruffled tuxedo and he'd make it look good.

"Everyone ready?" Evan asked, a big smile on his face as he looked at her.

"Yes, I'll meet you outside." Her pulse raced. Any time she got to see him, she had a hard time keeping it under control. No matter how many times she'd given herself her warning pep talk, it just didn't seem to stick when it came to Evan. She'd wear a goofy grin for days after being with him and she'd find herself thinking about him during times when she should be concentrating.

They headed down the sidewalk towards the Bartons'.

"So, Evan, have you decided what you'll be doing for school in the fall?" Abby asked.

Evan's cheeks reddened. "Not yet. I can't decide if I want to stay local or go back east. I'd really like to go to BYU for my graduate work but that all depends on which type of graduate work I choose. My parents want to make sure I choose the best school for that field, and that may not be BYU."

"Why don't they let you choose for yourself?" Abby asked.

"Probably they just have his best interests at heart," Sara said.

"Yeah, that," Evan said, though his voice wasn't exactly convincing.

"I'll probably just do everything here in Utah," Abby said. "I'm going to be a pharmacist and I don't see why I have to go to a far away school to get a degree. It will be just as good from University of Utah as it would be from NYU or University of Texas."

"Pharmacy. That sounds pretty cool," Evan said.

They reached the house and Sara went up the ramp the Barton's had set up for her.

"Come in, come in!" Crystal chirped when she answered the door. "And welcome back, Evan. It's a pleasure to see you again."

"Same," Evan said. "Thank you for inviting me."

"Anytime, especially if you come with Sara," Crystal said with a twinkle in her eye.

Sara sighed. Not hardly across the threshold and she was already started. She caught Evan's eye and he gave her an amused smile. At least he wasn't ready to make a run for the door—yet.

Todd came out from the kitchen and approached Evan. "So this is the famous Evan." He took the young man's hand and shook it. Sara wanted to crawl into a corner and start rocking back and forth. Everyone was bound and determined to embarrass her tonight.

"Evan, this is Crystal's husband, Todd Barton," Sara said, barely able to speak as her throat closed off. Her face was probably beet red by now. "This is Evan Farris, Todd."

"Farris, Farris," Todd said. "Do you happen to be related to Greg Farris?"

"Yes, he's my dad."

"Ah, I've done business with him," Todd said, nodding. "Fair dealer and has a good head for business."

"That he does," Evan said.

"Is everyone hungry?" Crystal asked. "Barbeque chicken is on the menu!"

They gathered around the table and after the food was blessed they ate the juicy chicken with corn on the cob and salad.

"You've really outdone yourself, Todd," Abby said. "This chicken is awesome."

"Thanks, hon," Todd said, beaming with pride. "It's my new Grillmaster."

"Todd and his grills," Abby said, chuckling.

"It's more man's best friend than a dog is," he said.

"So, Evan," Crystal said. "Are you still in school or are you working?"

"I'm technically still in school," he said. "I'm trying to decide on graduate school and then I'll probably get a job after that."

"Wonderful," Crystal said. "So important for a young man to have goals for his career so he can support a family."

"Crystal," Sara hissed.

"Do you like kids, Evan?" she continued.

"Yes, I plan on having some someday," Evan said, a grin crawling up his face as he looked at Sara's mortified face. "Just have to find the right woman to have them with."

"That is very important," Crystal said. "Someone sweet and patient and loving, and you know it never hurts if she's talented and smart."

If Sara thought she wanted to crawl into that corner earlier, she thought she'd need a rock now.

"I agree," Evan said, still looking at Sara. "I always thought the girl I'd marry would be someone I'd have a lot in common with. We'd have a lot to talk about and just enjoy each other's company."

Sara held her breath and looked down at her plate. She could feel the pressure of her heartbeat in her head.

"You know that's very true," Crystal said. "Todd and I, well, we're what you would call "opposites attract," and though it hasn't always been easy, we get along pretty well. But Sara and Abby's parents, Rebecca and Chris—they were birds of a feather. And once they met, it was pretty much over for the both of them. It was sweet, really."

"That's so cool to hear, Crystal," Abby said. "I mean, it's one of those things that Sara and I would see on a day-to-day basis but it was something we never really could put words to."

"Rebecca and I were more like best friends and sisters than cousins, Evan," Crystal said. "Up until she met Chris and I met Todd we pretty much were inseparable. I was so happy when she moved back to Utah so she could be around when Sara was born. She was such a beautiful baby too. Speaking of which—"

"No!" Sara said.

"What?" Evan said, sitting up.

"When we're done with dinner, I have something to show you," Crystal said, beaming.

"Oh, crap," Abby murmured.

They gathered in the sitting room and Crystal came back from her bedroom carrying two large picture binders.

"Oh, that's what you're talking about," Evan said, a huge smile across his face.

Sara transferred from her chair to the couch and wanted to hide her head under a pillow. Evan sat down next to her and squeezed her arm. The touch of his hand sent waves of warmth up her arm.

"I can tell her I'm really okay without seeing them, if you want," Evan said quietly to her.

Sara looked over into his large brown eyes. She had the sudden urge to grab his face and kiss him but she'd never do such a thing, especially not in front of everyone. He really was fantastic and thoughtful. Was it such a big deal? Probably not as much as she was making it out to be.

She shook her head. "I'm... . . . fine. It's just baby pictures."

"Are you sure?" he asked. "If you're uncomfortable with it, we can just do something else."

Her heart swelled. He was so sweet about it. "It's just that they keep pushing me on you and I don't want you to be uncomfortable. I mean this is the kind of stuff you show someone's boyfriend, you know?"

"Sara, I'm really okay with it. We're friends, right? It's the kind of stuff you'd show friends too. And if they push you on me, it just shows they care about you. Not that I mind too much."

Sara smiled at him. "You're being an awfully good sport about it."

"It's not that hard for someone I like," he said.

Crystal sat down on the couch next to Evan and opened up the photo album. "This is Rebecca and Chris. This is right after they got together—'97, I want to say. Still rocking that post-hippie look that was so popular back then. And this is when they came back to Utah. Look at that cute-as-a-button belly."

"You have your mom's hair, Sara," Evan said.

Sara nodded. She did. She was "her mom's little twin," everyone always said. She wondered if her baby bump would just be hidden by her lap, sitting in her wheelchair all the time like she did. If she had a baby.

"Oh, look at the little screamer," Crystal said after she turned a page. Sara put her head in her hand. "She really had a pair of lungs back then."

Evan chuckled.

Crystal showed him pictures of the rest of Sara's infanthood, and, trying to lean over to see what pictures Crystal was showing him, Sara found herself wedged in against his shoulder. It would have been so easy to rest her chin there, but she resisted.

"And this was when she was about four and a half. Terrible weekend," Crystal said, pointing to a picture of a little red-headed toddler. She lay in a hospital bed with IVs and monitor wires all over her. "She'd had the flu all week and we finally convinced Rebecca they needed to take her to the hospital. Her fever was so high. They admitted her right away and they were able to get her fever under control after a few hours. We were just about to take her home when she started complaining of back pain and tingles in her legs. Transverse myelitis."

"What's that?" Evan asked.

"It's an inflammation of the part of the spine as a complication of the flu. It's very rare, they told my parents, but I got it. So they were able to get it under control but not before my leg muscles were weakened and I lost some sensation in my legs as well."

He turned his head to look at her. Their faces were so close, she could feel his breath on her lips.

"I always wondered about that. I never had the courage to ask though. I thought it might be rude, or you might be offended."

"No," she said, giving him a sad smile. "I wouldn't have been. It's one of those weird random things that happen and I've learned to live with it. I really don't remember differently so it's always how I've been. But my parents and Crystal and Todd have been really cool and supportive."

"Sara's always been really independent, but, you know, Evan," Abby said, "the fastest way to tick Sara off is try to help her, unless you ask first, of course."

"Oh, so I might have gotten in really big trouble the other day, if I hadn't asked to help you with your chair then, huh?" he smirked.

"Yup, I'd have given you a dressing down better than any drill sergeant."

"I'll have to remember that," he said. In a quieter voice he said, "Maybe I'll do it anyway, just to see what an angry Sara looks like."

She shook her head, trying not to giggle. "You really don't want to see Angry Sara. Ask Abby about that later."

"Are you guys talking about me?"

"Yes, we were going to say we should have you bring Brandon next time," Sara said.

"Brandon? Who's Brandon?" Crystal asked.

Abby grimaced, giving Sara slitted eyes.

"He's just a friend—the kind that come by the dozen," Abby sang to herself.

They all laughed.

"Even if he's just a friend, you should bring him by, Abby," Crystal said.

"Maybe," Abby said, dragging out the syllables.

It was Sara's turn to give her a great big smile. Serves her right for encouraging Crystal when she should have been deflecting her instead. Sitting here with Evan she really shouldn't complain too loud. She felt so comfortable just leaning against him, feeling his warmth bleeding through his shirt, taking in the combination of the light scent of his cologne and his natural smell. And he didn't seem inclined to move or have her move as he watched Crystal flip the pages of the photo book.

"That's the Sara I remember," he said, pointing out a picture of Sara posing with her parents and Abby right after the Christmas concert. "Oh, look at that!"

Evan leaned in. "Holy cow, look." He pointed to a small point in the picture behind the group. "That's my parents right there so that must be me right there."

Sara leaned over further to look. Sure enough she could just make out Evan as she remembered him in high school talking to his parents. "I never noticed that."

And believe me, I would have been staring at this picture for hours back then if I had, Sara laughed to herself.

"Let me see," Abby said, coming over to look at the picture. "That is so crazy!"

She gave Sara a meaningful look. Sara gave her eye daggers. She knew exactly what Abby would say if Evan hadn't been sitting right there.

"No kidding," Evan said, leaning back in forcing Sara to sit back. "Except now that I'm looking at it, you haven't really changed all that much. Just a little older looking but definitely not in a bad way."

"We've all had to change a little bit since then," Sara said. "Seems like a lifetime ago, even though it's only been six years."

"Yes, things did change, that's for sure," Evan said, a sudden melancholy taking over his tone. "Sister and Brother Barton, I really appreciate the invitation to dinner tonight. The chicken was delicious."

"Anytime Evan. And you and Sara are welcome to come over whenever you want to practice. Just have Sara text me to give me a heads up, then come on over."

"I should probably get going home, but I've really enjoyed being here," he said, looking at Sara. His teasing, almost flirty mood was gone, replaced by something else, a sadness in his eyes. She would have loved to ask him about it but this certainly wasn't the place to do that.

"Did you want me to walk you to your car?" Sara asked.

"No, it's not that far," he said, getting up. "You stay here and enjoy your family. I'll see you guys on Sunday."

Abby gave Sara a questioning look and Sara shrugged.

"Nice to meet you, Evan," Todd said, holding the door for him and shaking his hand. "Give my regards to your dad."

"I will, thanks," Evan said. And then he was gone.

"I really like him, Sara," Crystal said. "Hang on to that one if you can."

"His family certainly makes enough money to make that worth her time," Todd said, sitting back down in his easy chair.

"That is not why I like him, Todd," Sara shot back.

"I know, I know," he said, placating her with his hands. "I'm just saying it would be a nice bonus."

Sara rolled her eyes. "He's very talented and smart and fun to be with. I'm just not certain he knows what he's doing with his life enough to make a commitment to anyone, much less consider me."

"I think you might be surprised, sweetie," Crystal said. "Sometimes, meeting the girl, the *one*, is the motivation a young man needs to get his priorities straight if he's been dragging his feet."

"Time will tell, I suppose," Todd said, looking at his wife. "I know you were my motivation. I may have known what I wanted to do already, but it sure gave me that kick in the butt to get things moving."

Sara sure hoped they were right, because she'd love to be able to have Evan look at her and say those three little words she'd dreamed of hearing. But the mixed signals she was getting from Evan made it seem like she'd have to just keep on dreaming.

CHAPTER 7

Abby paced on the sidewalk of the baseball diamonds at Riverton Park. She looked at her phone again. Brandon was late. That irritated her a little because she didn't like to stand around doing nothing. A nice-looking sedan rolled up in front of her and Brandon got out looking flustered.

"If anyone had told me that traffic would be so bad between Alpine and the Point of the Mountain, I would have considered buying a house in Lehi instead. I'm so sorry I'm late."

"I wondered," Abby said. "Shall we?"

They walked down the sidewalk a bit until they reached the grassy area beyond the baseball diamond. They didn't say much—Abby because she wasn't sure what to say. What did she have in common with Brandon anyway? Nothing? That was unfair. She barely knew the guy and he seemed content to just walk beside her.

"So tell me what you do at Adobe, was it?" Abby said finally.

"Yes. My team and I design and revamp the programs Adobe offers to their customers."

"Give me an example."

"Well, we have the number one software to read, create, and manipulate PDF files in the world, so we design upgrades to the programs and test them to ensure they work like they should. The idea is to innovate what we offer to customers."

"Nice," Abby said. "Sounds challenging."

"Yes, I suppose you could say that," he said. "But a very interesting challenge. And I've got a team of very talented people."

"I'm sure that helps."

"What about you?" he asked. "How much school do you have left?"

She gave him a side smirk. "Lots. I still have to get my undergraduate degree, probably in biology or chemistry. Then I have to do my graduate and doctorate work, then residency for another one to two years, and *then* I'll finally be a full-fledged pharmacist."

"Oh, wow," he said. "I guess it makes sense—you have to know as much about drugs as a physician does. Are you planning on being the local druggist at a grocery store?"

She shook her head. "If I can't find a good position as a researcher, I'd like to get a job at a big hospital so I can work with cancer patients."

"That I can understand based on what you said the other day."

They walked again in silence again. Brandon kept surprising her. She should have known that guys older than her would find her goals less intimidating than guys her age did. Like Will—he seemed to think that plans that definite were a commentary on his own lack of planning and initiative. Yet he never seemed to want to do anything with his life. He didn't have plans for a mission or college, and he seemed content with just working call center jobs. Not that there was anything wrong with that, but whenever she talked about her own plans, he tended to get antsy and change the subject to more mundane topics like clothes or movies.

Brandon, though, was different. Maybe it was because he'd been married before and was a father already. Or maybe it was because he had already gotten his degree and was putting it to good use in a job he obviously liked, or at minimum felt challenged by. That wasn't something you found everyday.

She also had to admit to herself that he was a pretty good-looking guy even if he wasn't exactly the type she normally liked. And there was something else about him. The way he looked at her didn't make her feel self-conscious. He looked at her like he liked what he saw, that he admired it—not like he was trying to decide if he wanted to look past what he saw to like her. That was a new experience for her.

"Do you mind telling me about your son Colin?" Abby said.

A smile spread across Brandon's lips. "He is a funny kid. He loves superheroes. He's very active and jumps off of everything trying to pretend he's flying. He's already an expert flirt, has all the girls in his classes at school charmed—including the teachers. He's super smart—too smart for his own good. That he got from me."

Abby nodded her head, giving him a half grin.

"I could go on all day, but he's just a really good kid and I miss him," he said, looking ahead of him as they walked.

"I imagine," she said. "I miss my parents. I'm glad I still have Sara and I'm glad we still have Crystal and Todd. But it's not the same."

"I imagine losing them so young allows you to know what you want at so young an age," Brandon said.

"Maybe," Abby said. "I think it just pointed me in the direction. I've always been goal oriented, and I knew what I wanted—but how I would get it was focused by their deaths."

"I can only imagine how hard that time must have been for you."

"Having good friends around helped me through the harder times. Will was always available to talk when I needed to vent. Sort of how it is now, except things seem to be changing as we get older and expectations are different."

"I imagine. Our expectations of ourselves should change as we get older. We should want better for ourselves. If there's one thing I've learned, it's that we have to make our own futures. We can't rely on our parents or other people to make it for us."

"That's something I know first hand," Abby said. "It's hard for some people my age to learn that because they rely on their parents so much. Like Will. I don't think he'd ever work if he didn't have to."

"That's not a very ringing endorsement of him," Brandon said. "It's hard to respect someone who lives for a bare minimum."

"I don't know if it's like that exactly," Abby said, feeling defensive. "He just doesn't quite know what he wants to do in life, so why should he waste energy on it?"

"My question is why not? Why not try and do as much as you can to figure it out? Why lay around and feel useless or dependent when you get so much more out of feeling like you're in control of your own destiny and path in life? You end up being told what to do by someone else that way. Maybe he likes it that way."

Abby shot him a look.

"I didn't really come here to talk about Will though," Brandon said. "He doesn't interest me nearly as much as you do."

"Now I know you're just trying to butter me up," Abby said.

"Why not?" he asked. "Isn't that the whole point? For me to get to know as much about you as possible?"

"I guess," she said. "There's really not all that much to know. I live with my sister. My parents are both gone and we live in a house that's owned by my mother's cousin. We're both trying to get through school and that's pretty much it. What about you? I know you've been married before, you have a little boy and you're from the Seattle area."

"That's the basics," he said. "My parents still live there, as well as my son and my ex. I moved out here because I needed a change of pace after the divorce. I miss my son so much, but I'll visit him as often as I can, but for now, I'm enjoying working for Adobe, even though it's only been about a month—and I've enjoyed the time I've spent with you and your sister."

"Well, there's that I guess," Abby said, giving him a small smile. "You seem pretty sure of yourself."

"I guess it would seem like that," he said. "I figure, what's the harm in going after a good thing? If it works out, I'm better off than I was before. If it doesn't, I'm no worse off than I was, and I can always try again."

"Huh," she said. "I never thought about life like that. I think it's because most people your age that I know are already married and settled. Not saying you're old or anything."

He chuckled, "Right."

"No, seriously. It seems like most people have it all figured out by the time they get to their mid-twenties, so I figured it would be the same for me—I'll be almost done with school and almost ready to work in my field. Treading my established course. But you—it sounds like you're sure of your decisions, but you're not being held down by them.

"I'll let you in on a secret," Brandon said. "Being my age--man, that makes me sound like I'm saying I'm so freaking old. But seriously, it may sound like I have it all figured out, but it still feels like I'm just as confused about what is going on around me as the day I graduated from college. That was right about the time my ex told me she was pregnant with Colin. Talk about a lot of decisions and responsibilities thrown at me at once. I don't know. It doesn't seem to get any clearer. Just the things you have to worry about get more complex."

"Please, make me feel even better about getting further into adulthood," Abby said, laughing.

"Sorry, I cannot tell a lie. Adulting sucks. It has its benefits, but it sure has its days when worrying about getting to school on time sounds like heaven in comparison."

Brandon held a chair out for Abby to sit down at the restaurant. Once seated, she pulled the napkin out and put it in her lap. Abby shook her head in surprise. She wasn't used to this kind of courtesy from a guy. It was sweet and sort of unnerving at the same time. Will never did this kind of thing, but she figured that was because they'd been friends for so long, it didn't occur to him that she'd like him to.

While they waited for the server, Abby fidgeted with her napkin. She wasn't sure what she wanted to talk about. Except maybe she did. There'd been a question forming in the back of her mind since they'd talked about Colin and Michelle that she wasn't sure she was brave enough to ask. Partly because she didn't want to give him the wrong idea, but the answer was burning her up with curiosity.

She tilted her head at Brandon. "Can I ask you a sort of off-the-wall question?"

"I like those," he said.

"As long as you don't take it the wrong way," she hurriedly amended.

He looked like he was trying not to laugh. "That I cannot promise since I have no idea what the question is."

She bit her lip. "Have you thought about getting married again?"

His eyes flew to hers. Yup, totally off the wall and completely unexpected.

"Um," he struggled. He reached up and scratched the back of his head. "I mean it's not something that's totally off the table. I'd have to be absolutely certain I'd met the right girl before I'd consider it again. Why?"

Now it was her turn to feel a little flustered. "Well, you just don't seem like the kind of guy who'd spend the rest of his life being a single dad. I mean I haven't known you that long but—" She shut her mouth. The rest of her sentence was supposed to be "it seems like you have a lot to offer a girl." The hole had been dug, and she was afraid she'd fall right in if she said it aloud.

"But?"

"Just that. You might want to consider it again."

He examined her as if he wasn't sure how to respond to that. "Thank you for your concern but I think I'll just keep going as I have been until I meet someone really special. I'm not in a rush to do anything at this point. Or is that what you're worried about?"

Abby blushed. "I've already told you what I expected for my life. I'm only nineteen. I'm at a place where that's not even something I'm thinking about yet. I've got too much school ahead of me and a career I want to get started."

"So you'd choose your career over potential happiness if it happened to drop into your lap a little early in your timeline?"

"Well, I wouldn't *not* consider it," Abby said. "I'm just not counting on it to happen that way."

"Why?"

"Because I'm not the kind of girl guys notice," Abby said, not able to look him in the eye anymore. She only looked back up when he hadn't said anything for a moment. He was looking at her like she'd said the most unbelievable thing ever.

"Oh, I see. You're just being modest. A fun and beautiful girl like you, and no other guy has noticed?" he scoffed.

"Beautiful?"

He gave her a look. "Yes, Abby, as if you didn't know."

Abby blushed. "Thanks. I did not know."

"Really?"

Abby looked away. She didn't want to have this conversation anymore. She knew he wasn't patronizing her but something about it made her mad and sad at the same time. Brandon's hand reached over the table and took hers. She looked at him and those deep blue eyes of his.

"I wasn't teasing you," he said, his brow furrowed. "I was completely sincere. I'm just having a hard time comprehending that no one, not one boy in that ward has tried asking you out."

She looked down at her hand in his. His hand was surprisingly soft. She licked her lips and took in a deep breath.

"I don't fit a certain mold," Abby said. "I won't ever. This is just how I am. Every girl that looks like me knows what I'm talking about because they've seen it happen to them too."

Brandon, with brow still furrowed, opened his mouth. "Because you don't look like a twig?"

Abby nodded.

He sat back in his chair, letting her hand go. He grimaced and put his hand up to his mouth. "I don't even know how to respond to that without coming off sounding like a total jerk or disingenuous."

"Then don't. I completely get it. What these guys see on TV, what they see in the movies, in magazines, online—it's all the same. And well, some of us don't look like that and never will, not unless we do some really unhealthy things to ourselves to look like that. I'm not willing to do that. So, I just get along the best I can."

#"But you should expect more than that," Brandon said, leaning forward. "I wasn't—okay, well I *was* trying to flatter you—but I wasn't exaggerating when I said you're beautiful. You are. Just the way you are. Any guy that can't see that is a moron."

Now Abby was sure her cheeks were crimson.

"Thanks, Brandon."

Brandon ran his hands down his face. "This conversation did not go like I expected."

"What did you expect?"

"I don't know—Coke or Pepsi? Red or black licorice? What's your favorite color?"

"Pink."

He smiled and chuckled. "Good to know."

"And yours?"

"Navy blue."

"Very specific."

"Well, there are a whole spectrum of colors in the universe. Some I like better than others. Just like there are a whole spectrum of body types and sizes and colors. Some I like better than others."

He gave her a meaningful look.

"And there are a whole spectrum of men's personalities. There are definitely some I like better than others," she said, giving him a smile.

CHAPTER 8

Abby put her jacket down on the front room couch when her cell phone rang.

"Hey, Will," she said. He always called her as soon as she got home from school. He sometimes knew her schedule better than she did.

"Hey, can I come over for a bit? Maybe we can go to the mall or something?" he asked.

"Yeah, sure," she said. "I've nothing better to do."

"You mean you don't have a date with Brandon?"

"As if you cared," she said, sighing. She watched out the window for Will's car. Now that he'd called it wouldn't take him long to be over. Sure enough, his car pulled into her driveway a few seconds later.

"Well, I don't really," Will said as he got out of his car out front. "I don't understand why you're going out with him."

"Because I like him," Abby said, standing up and opening the front door. "I'm not in love with him or anything, but I do think he's a nice guy and we have a good time when we're together. Not sure where you got the impression I didn't like him."

"It's not that I thought you didn't like him," Will said walking through her front door. He put his cell phone away and then plopped himself on her couch. "I meant that you just seemed lukewarm about him. I'm just surprised you've been on multiple dates with him."

"You're so annoying sometimes, do you know that?" she said, kicking his shoe. "If I didn't know any better, I'd say you were jealous. Just because I go on more than one date doesn't mean anything. You should know that better than anyone on this planet."

"What's that supposed to mean?" he asked.

"Uh, Mr. I-haven't-had-a-serious-girlfriend-ever. You only ever *date* them. You're never anyone's boyfriend, even if you date them longer than six months."

"Whatever, Miss I'm-too-picky," he said, pouting.

"Now what's that supposed to mean?" Abby said, folding her arms at him.

"*You* hardly *ever* date. There are tons of guys in the ward and yet all you do is hang out with me, as if no one else can compare. Now all of a sudden you and Brandon are merely 'date buddies.' Yeah, right."

"I don't date because no one ever asks me. Not because I'm picky. And I don't ask anyone out because I've known most of the guys in the ward since elementary school. Why would I ask one of those guys out? It would be like asking my brother out on a date, if I had one."

"So that's why you never asked me," Will said, rubbing his chin theatrically.

"Uh, no," Abby said. "I tried that already. Remember? It was junior year and I asked you to Girl's Pref and you said, and I quote 'I like you Abby, but only like a friend and I'll only ever like you as a friend.' Unquote."

"I said that?" Will asked.

"Yes," Abby said, giving him eye daggers. "Why? Have you changed your mind about that?"

Will thought about it for a minute, and for that sixty seconds Abby's heart sped up a little with hope. But he turned to her and with a teasing grin on his face.

"No, you know I haven't," Will said. "I like what we have. Besides, I think I'm going to start dating Olivia Farris a little more from now on. We went out last night."

Abby turned away from him so he couldn't see her pretend to gag into the kitchen sink. "Why her?"

"I don't know," he said. "She's pretty and she's fun to hang out with."

Yeah, right, Abby thought. "What did you guys end up doing on your date?"

"I took her to this ramen bar but we had to switch to a place with a salad bar because it didn't have any options that were vegetarian enough for her. Then afterwards I was going to take her mini-golfing, but it was too windy outside, so we ended up going to see a movie instead."

The whole time Will talked, Abby stood there trying not to laugh. When he saw her lips twitching, he gave her an annoyed look. "What?"

Abby couldn't help herself. "Seriously? She complained about where you took her?"

"Well, I didn't know she ate a certain way, so yeah, I changed restaurants. And I didn't mind going to a movie. We got to sit next to each other the whole time."

Abby rolled her eyes so hard she almost hurt them. "What a spoiled brat."

"Hey!" Will protested. "I wouldn't be talking so loud."

"If a guy was nice enough to plan a date to take me on, I would not whine about how windy it was."

"Well, she's not you, is she?"

"Yeah, I'm much less fussy than she is apparently," Abby said, shaking her head. "Heaven forbid her hair gets blown around. And you seriously want to date someone like her?"

"Someone like her?"

"Someone who's never going to be satisfied with anything you do unless you do it her way. High maintenance."

"I think you're the one that's jealous," he said, laughing. "You've only got Mr. Fluffy asking you on a date so you've got to put Olivia down so you don't have to feel so bad."

Abby sucked in a breath. That hurt. He'd never suggested she was desperate before. "You know, if you're going to be rude, you can leave," Abby said, marching up to him. She disliked Olivia so much at that moment. "I'd only be jealous of her if I was in competition with her, and you've told me plenty of times before that I'd never have a chance with you, so there is no competition. I was more worried about the fact that you're going to be running around like her little puppy dog on a leash doing whatever it is she wants you to do, and you're going to be so grateful she's letting you. But if that's the kind of relationship you want, congratulations on finding yourself the perfect woman to simp over."

Will stood up and for the first time in a really long time, he looked genuinely mad at Abby.

"I came over here to hang out but it's obvious all you want to do is insult me," Will said, walking by her. "I'll just go, since that's obviously what you want me to do."

"Nice one, Will. You're the one throwing insults around."

"Whatever, Abby."

He pulled the front door open and left, slamming it behind him.

Abby bit her lip. She wasn't necessarily sorry for anything she said. Everything she said was true, but she didn't like it when Will was mad at her. It took a lot for him to get mad at her, really mad, and now she felt like scum.

She went back into the kitchen to put the chicken she was making back in the oven when Sara rolled in through the garage.

"Was that Will I saw speeding down the road?" Sara asked.

"Yes," Abby said.

"What was his deal?"

"I made him angry at me," Abby said with a sigh. "He went out with Olivia last night and she was being a total brat but he accused me of being jealous because I was teasing him about it."

"Oh," Sara said, putting down her violin case and backpack. "Would it help if I said I don't really feel all that bad for him?"

Abby gave her sister a weak smile. "Maybe. Olivia was being terrible. She made Will change restaurants because she didn't like the food and then made him take her to a movie because she thought it was too windy to do something outside."

"Wow," Sara said. "Entitled much?"

"You're telling me," Abby said. "But Will doesn't see it like that. That was the part that was making me mad. He felt he was doing her some big favor by giving into her demands."

"Like I said, not sure I feel bad for him if he's going to act dumb like that," Sara said. "But those kinds of relationships are their own form of punishment, so hopefully he comes out of that haze soon."

"I don't even care if he does or not," Abby said, leaning against the kitchen counter. "I just don't want him to be mad at me. I don't even care who he dates normally, but he was so rude. Olivia is such a brat and I know it's because of her that he's acting like this. I guess I should have just kept my mouth shut. Sara, did you know he suggested I'm only going out with Brandon because he's the only one that would ask me out. That he's the only one that would be interested in me? Like Brandon and I are desperate, or something." Suddenly, tears welled up in her eyes.

"Abs," Sara said, coming up to her and hugging her around her waist. "No. Brandon's a good guy. He's not like Will and that intimidates Will. Any guy would be lucky to date you. Just because Will's too stupid to realize it doesn't mean that your worth is less because of it."

"I know. It's just the first time he's ever said something like that to me, and it hurt," Abby said, wiping away some of the moisture from her eyes.

"I bet he was just mad because there is some part of him that knows you're right but he doesn't want to admit it. So he does something totally immature and hurts you back."

Sara let out a quiet growl.

"I don't want to dog on Will too much. I know you care about him but it's this kind of stuff that makes me wish you wouldn't insist on being such close friends with him. He makes me so mad sometimes."

Sara's phone beeped. She pulled it out of the pocket under her wheelchair seat and looked at it. A big smile formed on her face. "It's Evan."

She wheeled into the front room. Abby looked after her and watched her texting back and forth with Evan for a while. The fact that Evan was contacting her outside of church and outside of their rehearsals gave Abby a warm feeling. Evan was quickly becoming one of Abby's favorite people even if he happened to share blood with one of her least favorite people. He was just so different from his sister. And the fact that he seemed to like Sara very much only gave him that many more bonus points.

"He's coming over tonight," Sara said. "I hope that's okay."

"Have him come for dinner," Abby said. "You never have to ask if it's okay if Evan comes over. He's invited anytime."

Seeing Sara's bright smile made Abby that much happier. "I will. You should text Brandon too."

"You think I should?" Abby asked. She wasn't sure. After what Will said, there was a part of her that thought that maybe she had encouraged him a little too much.

"Abby, don't listen to Will," Sara said. "Brandon, I think, genuinely likes you. He's not just dating whoever he can get his hands on. He really does like you."

"That's what I'm worried about," Abby said. "What if he likes me a ton but I don't like him as much?"

"Who says you have to start off liking each other the same?" Sara said.

"I don't know," Abby said. "I like spending time with him, but I don't know if I like him more than that."

"Has he complained about it?"

"No."

"Well, then don't worry about it. I mean, I'm far from an expert about relationships but I would imagine he's the kind of guy who'd say something about it if he's not okay with how things are."

"I guess so."

"Just call him. If he can't, he can't."

Abby pulled out her cell phone.

Come over for dinner with Sara and Evan and me?

It took him a little while to respond. It took so long she was almost sure he wasn't going to but just before she gave up, her phone pinged.

Sure, want me to bring anything?

She smiled. He was so thoughtful. That was something Will rarely was. If she invited him over to dinner, he just showed up.

You probably don't have time to do monster cookies so maybe just a pie or cake?

I can manage that. Favorite ice cream?

Cookies and cream.

Good call.

Abby giggled. And he had good taste in ice cream too. She found that she was sort of excited at the idea of Brandon coming over. Maybe it was just because she wanted to prove Will wrong about Brandon or herself. She wasn't desperate to date just anyone and, if what Sara said was true, neither was Brandon. She was picky, but not like that. If she had discovered on their first dates that she really didn't like Brandon's personality, she would have turned down further dates. But she found him to be intelligent and, maybe not hilarious, but at least funny enough to make her giggle once in a while.

She went down the hall to the bathroom to get spruced up before he got there.

Dinner went well and they were all sitting in the living room talking.

"Didn't you mention you had a house?" Abby asked.

"Yes," Brandon said.

"Nearby?"

"It's actually just a few streets down. Would you like to see it?"

Abby paused. Not that she thought Brandon would try anything, but the idea of suddenly being alone with him in a very private place like that was a little intimidating.

"I would but—"

"You don't want to come by yourself," he said for her. "How about everyone come then?"

"Where?" Sara asked.

"To my house," Brandon said. "I offered to show it to Abby. She's curious to see it."

"So am I," Sara said. "This will be fun."

"Evan and I can help you in, Sara," Brandon looked over at Evan and smiled.

"Yeah, sure I can do that," Evan said.

Abby went in Brandon's car and Sara went in Evan's. Abby looked behind them as they drove to Brandon's house.

"So any news on that?" Brandon said, tilting his head towards the other car.

"No. They've practiced together a few times, and my cousin invited him to dinner with us not too long ago but he hasn't made any moves yet."

"Hmm, he must be shy," Brandon said.

Abby laughed.

"What?" he said.

"'I know guys and that's not a polite nice,'" she said, imitating Brandon's deeper voice.

"Well, it wasn't," Brandon said. "Maybe he just likes to take things a little slower."

"Yeah, they can't all be as confident as you," Abby said.

"Exactly," Brandon said, giving her a grin. "But I still maintain that he likes her. "

"I agree. Or at least he's doing everything I know a guy does that likes a girl," Abby said.

"How am I doing?" Brandon asked.

"You are so . . . so cocky," she said, shoving his shoulder. "Wouldn't you like to know?"

"I would," he said, giving her a smirk.

They pulled up to a brown rambler in an older but well-maintained neighborhood. It was bigger than Abby's house with a nice green lawn in the front yard and a cute mini-picket fence.

"This is very nice," Abby said.

"Thanks. It's probably a bit bigger than I really need but it has a great fenced backyard and this is a really quiet neighborhood. Two big requirements I had besides being fairly close to my job. Shall we go in?"

"Yes," Abby said. She took in a breath. She didn't know why she should be nervous. It wasn't going to be her house. It's not like Brandon and she were getting married. She got out when Brandon opened the door for her. What would it be like to own her own home? Someday she would know. As a pharmacist, she'd make enough money to pick any house of whatever size she wanted. Decorate it however she wanted. And just call it her own.

Brandon got out his keys, unlocked the door and opened it.

"Alrighty, Sara, I've got you," Evan said, lifting her up. "And Brandon, can you grab her chair?"

Brandon and Abby gave each other a grin as Evan lifted Sara into the house. Once inside, Abby looked around. There was minimal furniture for a house that looked much bigger on the inside than the outside. Definitely a bachelor pad. There were no walls separating the kitchen and the living room. She could see straight through the room into the backyard. She walked towards it while Sara looked around the rest of the house. There was a large wooden swingset set up and lots of green space for running around.

"I could almost see a white lab running around back here," Abby said, mostly to herself.

"If I could be home more, that would be a great idea," Brandon said, coming up to stand next to her. "But since it's just me, it'd be unfair."

"I understand,"

"Are you a dog person?"

"I'm a whatever person," Abby said, shrugging. "Except maybe rodents, or scaly things. Not a big fan of those."

"This would be a perfect space for a party, Brandon," Sara said.

"And if I had more friends than just you guys, I'd say that would be a fantastic idea," he said, turning around. "A barbeque in the backyard, maybe?"

"That sounds like a lot of fun. Let's do it this Saturday," Abby said. "BYOM and have everyone bring a dessert?"

"How about BYOM and we make assignments for the rest so we don't have twenty desserts and no chips or soda?" Sara asked.

"What is this BYOM? Is it like BYOB?" Brandon asked.

"Bring your own meat," Abby said.

"Oh! Yeah, that will make the party a little cheaper," Brandon said. "And everyone brings something to share—so a potluck, even though it's just a few friends?."

"I guess?" Abby said, looking at Sara. "It's just how we've always done it. It spreads the responsibility around so that no one person is trying to guess how many mouths they'll have to feed. You just never know how many people are going to show up."

Brandon raised his eyebrows. "Why is that statement not exactly reassuring?"

CHAPTER 9

Sara checked her phone and found texts from Evan and Brandon. The text from Evan read:

This should be fun tonight
Can't wait to see you there

The one from Brandon read:

I got all the priesthood brethren
I'm assuming you got the sisters
Is this just a big glorified ward activity?

Sara giggled. Brandon wasn't wrong. But he didn't really know anyone here in Utah, and while Sara and Abby had invited a few people they knew outside the ward, and Evan and Will had too, the majority of the people coming to the party at Brandon's house were all from the singles' ward.

And then there was Evan. She couldn't help the happy sigh. They'd had another rehearsal at Crystal's house and once again it was like playing in heaven with him. It was quite apparent that neither one needed the extra practice. They were perfectly in sync as far as the music was concerned so really it was an excuse to get together during the week but for something that wasn't classified as a date. He was adamant about that, for some reason. He just said he wasn't going to date anyone this summer for the reason Abby warned Sara against getting attached to him—he'd be leaving mid-August.

Problem was, it was too late for that. She tried not to think about it. It was only June so there was still time.

Sara texted Brandon back:

> *Abby and I are on our way*
> *see you in a min*

Then she sent a text to Evan:

> *Looking forward to seeing you too*

She was seriously tempted to type out stuff like, "I really like you. Do you have to have that ban on dating? Could we hang out more during the week? Could you carry me off to the temple for time and all eternity?" She wouldn't of course but it was fun to think she might.

Abby walked into the room. She wore an adorable pink sundress with matching strappy high heels.

"Aren't you worried that you're going to sink into the grass?" Sara asked.

"No, you walk on the balls of your feet when you walk on soft surfaces," she said, smoothing out her dress.

"Oh, I guess that makes sense. Sort of."

"Oh, ye of the uninitiated," Abby said.

Sara rolled her eyes. "I see very little point in wearing high heels in my situation. Flats do very well and can be just as cute."

"Keep telling yourself that," Abby said. "Let's get out of here. I want to get there early to help Brandon set up."

"You seem to have formed a much better opinion of him since that date," Sara said, as they got in the car.

"I have," Abby said. "I'm not going to lie and say I haven't. He's very nice. Very smart. It doesn't hurt he called me beautiful."

"Really?"

"Yes," Abby said, flipping her long blonde hair over her shoulder.

"Promising," Sara said.

"I'm not saying he's ready to propose tomorrow, or that I would say yes if he did, but we had a nice time and I enjoyed getting to know him better. Let's not put a label on it just yet."

"If you say so," Sara said, trying to hide her smirk. She was certain Abby was trying to downplay how much Brandon's stock had risen, or how much her interest in him had increased. Based on what she'd observed of him, if he wasn't head over heels for Abby already, he was pretty close. Sara was glad. She liked Brandon, platonically, and his steady, easy-going personality would be a perfect counterpoint for Abby's social-butterfly, sometimes insecure personality. She just had to wait and see.

They pulled up to Brandon's house and Sara was more than pleased to see Evan waiting outside. When he saw them pull up, he turned and knocked on Brandon's door. Brandon appeared and he paused for a moment when he saw Abby step out of the car. Sara could swear she saw Abby blush as Brandon took in Abby's dress and heels. He didn't say anything but smiled at her. Just like last time, Evan put Sara in his arms and Brandon grabbed her chair.

As he carried her, he looked over and gave her a big smile which sped her heart rate up significantly. "You're very kind to do this, you know."

"I didn't even think about it," he said, as he placed her in her wheelchair. A flicker of disappointment swept her chest. She liked the feeling of his arms around her and the moment was all too brief. "I'm happy to anytime."

Her heart skipped a beat and she had to pull in an extra deep breath to compensate.

"So, Brandon, what can we do to help?"

The next hour or so they set the house up for company and little by little the front room filled up with people from the ward. The house was noisy, but it was a good noisy. At some point, Sara lost track of Evan and she contented herself with sitting with a circle of girls from the ward as they gossiped about the latest couples in the ward and speculating on which ones were getting engaged next.

A loud chorus of laughter came from the backyard lawn. Sara turned and saw a group of boys standing around talking to each other. She saw Will practically in the middle of it. She grimaced. They way they laughed, whatever they were talking about couldn't be good. She also noticed Brandon and Evan stood nearby but not quite a part of the circle talking to each other. She turned and went towards the back door. Abby came up behind her.

"What's going on back there?" she asked.

"No idea," Sara said. "Whatever it is, Will's knee deep in it."

"That sounds pretty typical."

The group laughed again and Evan and Brandon both walked away both with grimaces on their faces.

Sara backed up into the kitchen to allow them room to come in.

"It's not right," Evan was saying. "I probably should have said something."

"Just leave it," Brandon said. "They're a bunch of idiots."

"What's going on?" Abby demanded, hands on her hips.

"Are you sure you want to know?" Brandon said, folding his arms across his chest.

"Is it bad?" Sara asked.

"Yes," Evan said.

"Then, yes."

"Apparently, they have a rating system for the girls in the ward."

"A what?" Abby asked, flabbergasted.

"A rating system. For how datable a girl is," Brandon said, giving Abby a particularly significant look. "I'm sorry, Abby. I really didn't believe you until today."

All Abby did was bite her lip.

"What is this rating system based on?"

"I don't know . . ." Evan said.

"No, I want to know."

Evan sighed. "How tall she is, what size she is, how well she does her hair and makeup, clothing style, physical disfigurements like moles, freckles, scars and disabilities," Evan said, flinching at the last one. "Skin color, intelligence, and how easily she'll kiss you."

Sara's jaw dropped open. "So specific," she said, swallowing. She felt water pooling in her eyes. She thought she hadn't liked Will before. She licked her lips, and looked up at Abby. She was looking out the door at Will still with the crowd of boys. "I, uh, don't know what to say."

"Don't say anything," Evan said. "It's ridiculous and mean. Any man that would decide who to date based on it wouldn't be worth wasting your time on."

"The problem is you don't know which ones do," Abby said.

"That circle gives you a pretty good idea," Brandon said, looking over his shoulder at Will and the rest of the guys standing there.

"Would you guys excuse me just a moment, please?" Abby said. She swept past Brandon. They all watched as she marched up to Will, took his arm and steered him out of the backyard.

"He's in trouble," Sara said. "Good. He needs a good slap upside the head. Not that it will do any good long term. She always forgives him eventually."

"He's not worth it," Brandon said. "I don't understand."

"Neither do I," Sara said. "And I've known him since he moved here. He hasn't changed much since we've known him, he's always treated Abby like she's second tier, yet she still insists on being friends. I wish there was something I could do or say that would change her mind."

"Me, too," Brandon murmured.

"Just keep trying," Sara said. "Maybe she just needs to be shown there are men out there that will treat her with the respect and attention she deserves. I mean, I don't want you to feel like you're beating your head against a wall, but I don't think it's a total lost cause."

Brandon looked down at her for a moment and then walked off.

Sara sighed.

"He really likes her doesn't he?" Evan asked.

"Yes, I think he really does," Sara said. "I think Abby likes him too, but he scares her. Will's safe because she's known him forever and he gives her just enough attention to make her feel important to him, but not enough to think he'd ever be interested."

"That's . . . that's," Evan said. "I'm not even going to judge it. It's not my place."

"Then you're better than I am," Sara said, laughing.

"You're her sister," he said. "I think you're entitled to have an opinion in the matter."

"Sure, but that doesn't mean I hold any weight when it comes to what she feels. She's going to have some very rough decisions coming up in the next few years and I can advise her, but she has to make the decision."

Evan had rested his chin on his chest. He was silent for a moment. "Do you want to go sit outside on the patio?"

"Sure," she said. She followed him and they sat near each other at the table under the canopy. They were far enough away from the group of men that they could talk without having to shout.

"I wish my family felt the way you do," Evan said.

"What do you mean?"

"One of the reasons I'm having such a hard time deciding what to do for graduate school is because I don't like the options they're giving me."

"Wait, what?" Sara said, sitting up a little straighter. "You don't get to pick your own graduate degree?"

"Sort of, sort of not," he said. He looked embarrassed. "Maybe I shouldn't have said anything."

"Oh . . . no, Evan," Sara said, placing her hand over his. "I wasn't judging you. I'd just never heard of that before. What do they want you to do?"

He turned his hand over and held hers, and rubbed her fingers with his thumb.

"Well, the deal is, I pick one of the degree programs they want me to pick and they pay for all of it—tuition, room and board, expenses, books and fees, everything. No matter where it is."

Sara had a hard time concentrating on what he was saying because the touch of his hand was making her stomach do flips.

"That's a very generous offer," she said, her voice hitching a little. "What do they want you to pick from?"

He grimaced when he looked up at her. "MBA, Political Science, Medicine, or Law."

She tried to not let her jaw drop open, so she bit her lip instead. "Um, wow. Those sound like very involved degree programs."

"They are," he said, nodding. "I wouldn't do well at a single one. My heart wouldn't be in any of them."

"Then why not let you make your own choice?"

"That is the question of the hour, isn't it?" he said, giving her a sad smile. "It's because anything else wouldn't make enough money and isn't a profession prestigious enough for a Farris man."

Sara sat back, stunned. "I honestly thought those kinds of families only existed in nine-teenth century novels and soap operas."

"Welcome to my family," he said.

"What do they expect Olivia to do? Let me guess—marry well?"

"Yes."

This time Sara couldn't help but her mouth dropping open. "I was kidding. Seriously?"

He nodded. "They want her to find a nice rich Mormon boy who has connections to the more important families in Utah and California. They thought they had sealed the deal with Cameron Matheson, but he got accepted to Duke University to play football and earn a research scientist degree. He broke up with her right before he left, so now she has to start over."

"But she's been after Will. Will's family isn't wealthy or well-connected."

Evan shrugged. "As long as all she's doing is playing, they don't care, I guess. But if he tried to propose to her, it'd be a different matter altogether."

"Abby would be happy to hear that," Sara said.

"Why? Is she in love with Will?"

Sara nodded.

"Oh. Now I get what's going on. That's why Brandon's so irritated with the kid."

"I just think Abby needs a change of scenery. Will's not the best friend she's ever had but she clings to him like he has been. I think she likes the idea of being in love with Will, rather than actually being in love with him. But he's told her very clearly, he doesn't see her that way. But she hopes anyway. And she gets her heart re-broken every time he dates someone new."

"Dating sucks," Evan said.

"Not if you're dating the right person," Sara said.

"I wish I had the time to find out," Evan said as he examined Sara's face, then let go of her hand.

Every time he moved forward just a little, he backed up. It was so frustrating. But at least this time, he'd confided something in her. That was definitely a step in the right direction. She couldn't imagine her own parents acting the way his parents did. They had always been Sara and Abby's biggest cheerleaders in whatever they'd wanted to do. To know that your parents' support was conditional must be awful. And more than that, awful for a guy who was one of the sweetest and most kind people she knew. Why not just let him pick whatever it was he wanted to do? So what if he didn't want to be a doctor or a lawyer? She didn't understand that mentality at all.

CHAPTER 10

Sara finished up the last of the pork chops and stirred the gravy. She and Abby had invited Brandon over for dinner. Sara had invited Evan too but he couldn't come—his family required his presence at some dinner party. Since the conversation she'd had with Evan about his family's expectations, she wondered if Olivia wasn't the only one expected to marry well. Was there any doubt? If they had so much sway over his education, of course they'd dictate his relationships, too. So, it would stand to reason that these mandatory dinners served another purpose, other than enjoying gourmet cuisine. She still couldn't wrap her head around the idea that such an antiquated custom was still being practiced. Back then it was almost a societal requirement; today it was heavy-handed manipulation.

A knock at the door brought her out of her thoughts.

She hurried to answer the door when the knock came and Brandon stood there.

"Come on in," she said, smiling.

"Hello," he said.

"Abby should be out in a minute," she said. "I'm just finishing up the last part of dinner."

"Need help with anything?" he asked.

"You could probably get some place settings out," Sara said. "Set the table."

"That is easy enough."

"Only three today though."

"Where's Evan?"

"He had a family obligation today," Sara said. "So it's just us."

"I hope he's having the time of his life," Brandon said with a sardonic smile.

"I'm thinking probably not, poor guy."

Abby came around the corner. "Hi, you look nice."

"Just a t-shirt and jeans."

She shrugged. A slight blush spread across her cheeks, and Sara tried to keep her smile to herself. Things had been developing slowly . . . but they were developing between Brandon and Abby—and Sara was glad. She really wanted Abby out from under Will's thumb, and Brandon was a really good guy. It seemed like the more time they spent together, the more Abby liked Brandon. Sara couldn't be happier. She wasn't sure Abby was ready to admit it out loud—maybe not even to herself—but Sara knew her sister well enough to know that something was stirring.

They sat down to dinner and about halfway through Brandon spoke.

"The last few times I've been here, particularly since the party at my house, I've been looking around. I think my house is a little sparse, but you guys have your house looking like a home."

"Thank Sara for that. Miss Suzy Homemaker over there can sew, picked out all the curtains, and planned where to put up the pictures. She's really great at it."

Sara shook her head. "Yeah, but I needed your sense of style, too. I might have chosen that calico fabric if you hadn't stopped me."

"True. I did rescue us from that."

"I guess I'm glad Evan's not here tonight. I might lose some guy cred if I asked you a favor in front of him."

"I doubt that, but what's up?" Sara asked.

"I was wondering if you might help me make my house look less like a bachelor pad and more like a home. Would you ladies be up for that?"

"That sounds like an interesting challenge," Sara said. "What do you think, Abby?"

Abby's cell phone rang.

"Be right back." She stepped away from the table, but was still close enough that Sara and Brandon could hear what she was saying. "What? Seriously, Will, I'm in the middle of dinner. Yes, he's here. I'm pretty sure we've had this discussion before . . . What? Fine. But after dinner. Whatever. Bye."

Sara arched an eyebrow at Abby.

"Seems Will's having a jeans existential crisis but his mom left his keys and he really needs to go to the mall."

"On Sunday?"

"I'm only going to take him there and back. It shouldn't take very long. I won't be buying anything."

Sara sighed. She glanced at Brandon. He looked down at his plate but he looked annoyed.

Abby quickly ate the rest of her food. "I can't imagine I'll be longer than an hour." And with that she grabbed up her purse and keys and was out the door.

Sara started to gather the plates off the table.

"Let me get those, please?" Brandon stood up and held his hands out to grab the dishes from her.

"I'm doing the dishes though because otherwise I'm going to say some not very nice things and I really don't want to go there on a Sunday."

"You, too, huh?"

"Practically since day one," Sara said, as she emptied out the dishwasher. "I mean he's a nice enough guy at first glance. But the way he treats Abby . . . He treats her just nice enough that she'll stick around, and then he'll throw tantrums with her to get what he wants. Then she feels guilty because she thinks it's her fault. I've talked until I'm blue in the face about him but she won't listen."

"So, you're saying I have no chance with her?"

Sara looked at Brandon. "Actually, I was thinking the exact opposite. She's had her head up in Will's cloud for so long that I think she's forgotten there are other guys out there—nicer guys—that act their age and will treat her well all the time."

Brandon gave her a half smile.

Sara fought with herself. Abby's personality for the most part was pretty steady. She was loyal and kind-hearted. But when it came to romance, she'd had so little experience, Sara worried that a well-meaning guy like Brandon might find himself caught up in a drama that was more appropriate for junior high kids, especially where Will was concerned. But at the same time, she'd seen the way her sister looked at Brandon. She wondered if it would be a betrayal of sorts to tell Brandon this, especially since encouragement could end up nowhere.

"I think you're growing on her, Brandon," Sara said carefully. "I can't make any guarantees, but she's different around you now. And I'm not just saying this because I'm her sister and I'm talking her up. I really do like you as a person and I'd like to see you happy, too."

"That is very kind of you, Sara. I like you too."

"I would tell you if I felt like there was no chance for you," Sara said. "I just have to make sure that I'm as honest as I can be with you without betraying my sister's trust. That's my priority."

"Fair enough."

"So, about your house, I have some homework for you," Sara said.

"Homework?"

"You didn't think I'd do it all for you, did you?"

The look on his face said that maybe he did. "Okay, homework."

"I'll be right back." She got her laptop and brought it out to the kitchen table. "Your homework is to do the following: Pick your favorite color, maybe two. Pick one neutral color—white, black, gray, brown, tan. Then you're going to find pictures on the internet of different design elements like window coverings, decorations, photo frame displays, paint colors; or, they have entire room models set up that you can choose from. Then we'll go through and pick out what you like the best and order what you need for your space."

"It sounds like a lot, but at the same time, really too easy."

"It's not hard."

Brandon nodded. He sat and thought for a moment. "As a friend, can I ask you a question?"

"Sure."

"Has Evan ever asked you out on an official date?"

"No," Sara said. "He refuses to call when we go out together *dates*."

"Huh," Brandon said, scratching his beard.

"What?"

"Just . . . I'm usually right about this kind of thing."

Sara gave him a confused look. He returned it with a sheepish grin.

"I mean, it's no secret he likes you," he said.

Sara could feel the blush creep up her cheeks.

"And when a guy likes a girl that much, they usually don't wait around to call it what it is."

"Which is?"

"Like."

Sara laughed.

"Well, *like* made a little more *official* with official dates, that is."

"I guess I figured he doesn't want to lead me on because he'll be leaving in August."

Brandon nodded in agreement. "I suppose you're right. It's too bad. You never know. He could change his mind."

"Don't do that. I have a hard enough time keeping my mind on the present and just leaving it in the Lord's hands."

"Well, He has this marvelous way of positioning things so that everything works out like it should."

"I hope you're right," Sara said. "Evan's a good man and any girl would be lucky to have him in her life."

"Yup, including a certain red-head who's had a crush on him since high school. Yeah, Abby told me."

"Well, this red-head isn't holding her breath—I'd probably suffocate before anything happened. Of course, I'm sure his mother would love that."

"Is she that scary?"

"Yes. Imagine Olivia in about twenty-five years and looking like she sucked on a lemon."

"I have no words for that."

"It's just amazing that a woman like her raised a son who's as kind and thoughtful as Evan is."

"Takes all kinds, I guess."

"Please, Brandon, I appreciate you talking to me, but don't say anything to Evan. I don't want him to think I'm waiting around for him. He's under enough pressure already. I just try to be content with the time we have together because I know the summer won't last forever."

"I won't say anything to him. We're friends, I'd say, but he's not very forthcoming about himself, so even if I wanted to, I couldn't tell you much more than what I've guessed."

"Thanks, I appreciate that."

Abby took a bit longer to get back than she said she would, so Brandon and Sara spent the rest of the time talking about Colin and his job. She'd never had a male friend before. She'd been too shy in high school, plus Will had ruined her on the idea of it. But Brandon was easy to talk to and it was nice to have a male perspective on this. When Abby did finally walk back in the door, it was obvious by the way her face lit up when she saw him that, even though she was willing to leave for Will, she still looked forward to seeing Brandon. It gave Sara hope that Will's grip on Abby was finally slipping.

CHAPTER 11

Sara waved when she saw Evan pull up into her driveway. She held her sandals in her hand. She planned on putting them on when they got to the Center. Before then she wanted the sun on her toes.

"What a beautiful day!" she said as he got out of his car. "It's going to be perfect to watch a concert."

"I agree," he said, looking up at the blue and cloudless sky. "Do you have an umbrella?"

"Uh, no," she said.

"I was going to bring one because I'm prone to sunburn, but even more for you, Miss Red-Head," Evan said, as he got her wheelchair in his car. "Let's stop by my house. I have an umbrella there we can use. It won't make us too late, I don't think."

Thinking of going to Evan's house made her feel a little sick. It's not like she got the warmest welcome the last time she was there. But since he was probably only just going to run in the house and run back out she willed herself to relax.

"So, Gallivan Center, and the group is doing Vivaldi's Seasons?"

"Yes."

"I'm so excited. I love Fall so much. It's so much fun to play."

"Is it?"

"Oh, yes. It's bright and cheerful and challenging."

"You'd think Fall would be sort of somber."

"Yeah, but I think Vivaldi was trying to celebrate the beauty of each of the seasons rather than use a classic interpretation of them. I like it better this way."

"Do you know what we should do next?"

"What?

"We should try to find something by Mozart, like a violin/piano arrangement of one of the violin concertos. Do something a little more challenging than a hymn."

"I like that idea. It's too bad we wouldn't have time to do that before you have to leave for school."

"Ah, yes," he said. His face fell a little. "I forget about that sometimes."

"I wish there was a way you could change their minds."

"Me, too," he said, giving her a wan smile. "So, now to choose which one I would hate the least."

"I'd laugh but it's really not that funny," Sara said.

They pulled up into the Farris family driveway. She looked up at the grand house. She kept forgetting how huge it really was. More than enough room for the four people living there to never see each other.

"I have an idea," he said. "How about you come in for a minute and meet my family? Looks like everyone is home."

She didn't want to hurt Evan's feelings but if there had been any way she could have gotten out of it, she would have said no. He had such a hopeful look in his eyes that she relented. She hoped maybe this time his mother would be more friendly—or maybe his dad was.

"Okay, grab my wheelchair and I'll put my sandals on really quick."

Evan made quick work of putting her wheelchair together and parking it next to her seat before he went to open the front door of his house. Sara was attempting to get her toes through the straps when she heard someone come outside with keys in their hands. She looked up and saw Olivia walking towards Evan. Since her door was open, she could hear the brother and sister talking.

"What's she doing here?" Olivia asked in a sour voice.

"We're going to a classical concert downtown," Evan said. "I needed to pick up the game umbrella and thought maybe I'd introduce her to Mom and Dad."

"You're taking her on a date?" Olivia sounded shocked.

"No, it's not a date. We're friends. I'm not dating, remember?"

"Looks like a date. You could do so much better, Evan. There are so much better-looking girls in the ward—and ones that can actually walk."

Sara bit down on her lip so hard she was afraid she might have drawn blood. She rested her head against the dashboard and got her breathing and the moisture pooling in her eyes under control. It wasn't a huge surprise to hear Olivia say something like that. She'd never liked the girl either but it hurt to hear her say that out loud.

"I'm not dating right now, and I don't see what difference it makes if she can walk or not if she's a nice, intelligent, talented person. She doesn't have to wear pounds of make-up to look beautiful. She just naturally is. Pardon me for being a bit more picky with my friends than you are. I like them to be able to communicate without their cellphones."

"Whatever, Evan. Mom's going to eat her alive."

Sara's whole frame shook and she was torn between feeling insulted for what Olivia said, and overjoyed by how Evan defended her.

"Are you okay?" She looked up and saw Evan watching her in concern.

"I think so," Sara said, sitting back up.

"You heard that, didn't you?"

"Yes, but I wasn't surprised to hear it come out of her mouth," Sara said. "She's always disliked Abby, so I assumed she disliked me by default."

"Ready to go inside?" Evan asked. "Or maybe I should just go myself."

"No, I'll be fine. I've already met your mother. She didn't intimidate me then—I doubt she'll do any worse this time." She gave him an encouraging smile.

"Okay, if you feel you want to," Evan said.

"I do. It's your family. It's only fair since you had to endure mine."

"Endure." He laughed. "You have a way with words, Sara."

He helped her over the bumpy threshold and escorted her into the house. The foyer was at least three stories high with a large wrought-iron chandelier hanging from its apex. The colors were rich and dark, sort of like Evan's mother's coloring. The foyer opened up into a massive great room complete with fireplace, several sitting areas, a big screen TV nearly the size of a movie theater screen, and a gourmet kitchen that looked big enough to have its own staff to man it.

"Do you like it?" he asked.

"It's huge," Sara said.

"Yes, it is."

She wandered over to the kitchen and looked in the large commercial double ovens. "I could make a turkey, dressing, rolls, and six pies all at the same time in these," Sara laughed. Then she ran a hand over the massive commercial refrigerator. "I think a family of four lives in here, don't they?"

Evan smiled at her. "Probably. I'll go get my parents."

Sara looked around. She hadn't wanted to show Evan, but the house was intimidating all by itself. Everything in the kitchen was big and expensive. Everything in the great room was luxurious and orderly. The couches were made of the softest leather. She went to look out the large picture windows that lined the back wall of the house. Even the backyard was grandiose and extravagant. Water features spilled down rock pathways that led into mini Japanese buildings and a rock garden. The patio was set out with tons of chairs and loungers surrounding a pool. Evan's dad certainly did well for himself. It was overwhelming.

"Sara," Evan said. She turned around. She recognized Evan's mother right away. Nothing had changed about her but her clothes. Evan's father looked exactly as she'd imagined. He was an older version of Evan—the kind face with similar features, but with graying temples and smattering of salt and pepper in the rest of his hair. But he, too, did not smile when he saw her.

"Mom, Dad, this is my friend, Sara Larsen," he said, a big smile on his face. "Sara, this is my dad, Greg and my mom, Jennie."

"It's nice to meet you both," Sara said, hoping her smile looked genuine even though her hands shook. "Brother Farris, my cousin is Todd Barton. He says he's done business with you before. Todd is like a second father to me."

"Yes—Todd. I remember him. Where did your first father go?"

"Um, both my parents have passed."

"I see. And what do you do, Sara Larsen?"

"I'm in school right now, on my last semester. I have a double major in art and music. I'm a portraitist and illustrator, and I also play violin with the university orchestra."

"A very unreliable profession, art and music," Greg said.

"I suppose that depends," Sara said. "I've already got a small portfolio doing illustration commissions online and once I graduate, I plan on taking violin students to supplement my income. Once I'm not in school I'll have more time for commission work."

"With a mountain of student debt, no doubt," he said.

"Actually, no," Sara said, flexing the muscle in her jaw. So, he was going to constantly belittle her choice of profession just because it wasn't something he found worth in, was he? "My parents had college funds set up for me and my sister, and we've both managed not to accrue any debt. My sister won't take on any for pharmacy school, either."

She looked at Evan. There was anxiety in his eyes but also pride.

"We really should get going," Evan said. "I'll grab that umbrella really quick."

#Once Evan left the room, both his parents took a step forward. Sara felt like a pack of hyenas was circling her.

"Our son is getting ready for graduate school," his mother said. "He doesn't need any entanglements or reasons to shirk his duty, least of all with someone whose care needs will cost him so much."

"Sister Farris, Evan's already told me all this himself," Sara said. "I'm not here to get in his way. I'm just his friend, and support him in whatever decisions will make him happiest. I'm sure as his parents you feel the same way—that you want him to find a career that will make him happy."

"I assure you, whichever career path he chooses, he will be happy," Jennie said. "Happy that he doesn't have to struggle to pay his bills or provide for his family. Did he tell you that if he chooses against our wishes, we won't pay for his schooling?"

"He did," Sara said.

"Then he may or may not have told you that if he decides on a more foolish career path, he will have to learn his life lessons the hard way, because we won't support it. He wouldn't get a penny from us."

"I understand," Sara said. "You've raised an intelligent, talented man. I'm sure he'll manage without it, if he chooses that course."

"Shall we go?" Evan asked from behind his parents. "We don't want to be late."

"It was a pleasure to meet you both," Sara said as she wheeled by them.

Once Evan closed the door, she took in a deep breath. She hurried to get into the car. Evan put her wheelchair in the car, got in, started the car and then pulled her into a tight hug. She hugged him back.

"Did you mean that? What you said?"

"Not sure what you heard—your parents were kind of in the way, but everything I said, I meant."

He let go of her and pulled out of the driveway. "Thank you. I'm not sure what to say besides that. I really just appreciate your support."

Sara looked at him and smiled. "Of course. You should be able to choose what makes you happiest in life. I know choices come with consequences. All our choices, good and bad. But the decisions we make for ourselves teach us the most, not the ones that are made for us.

"I understand where your parents are coming from. They don't want you to struggle. Being poor isn't glamorous—but it's not shameful either. You make do with what you have, and appreciate better things when you get them."

"Have I told you recently how amazing you are?" Evan said. "Seems like every time you've done something to impress me, you turn around and do something even better."

Sara felt the heat in her cheeks. "Don't put me up on a pedestal, Evan. I'm not perfect. I make mistakes too. I just try to do better next time and repent when I can."

"All I can say is you're one of the best friends I've ever had," he said, taking her hand in his. "And I'm sure if my friends were perfect, they certainly wouldn't want to be friends with me."

"Anyone who knows you would want to be friends with you," she said, letting the warmth of his hand crawl up her arm and straight into her heart.

Once they got settled at the Gallivan Center, they sat side by side under the umbrella. She was glad they stopped for it, even if she had to spend those nerve-wracking seven minutes at Evan's house. The sun wasn't so gentle or nice after sitting directly under it after a while.

The chamber orchestra played through the seasons and Evan and Sara continued to hold hands. She thought about Evan. Was it possible to feel more for him than she already did? She knew two things deep inside. He was attracted to her—everything he did, every time he texted her, every time they talked, every time they smiled at each other, it was there. And she was scared to death of the day when he'd come to her and say he had to leave. She hadn't seen him in the six years before this. That seemed like an eternity. How long would it be, if ever, before she saw him again if he left? And maybe he'd forget about her in the meantime, find another girl, and her chance with him would be over. She shivered thinking about it.

"Are you cold?" he whispered to her.

She looked over and was surprised to see how close his face was to hers. They stared into each other's eyes for so long, time seemed to slow down. His eyes once dipped down to her mouth and her lips parted with a little gasp. Was he going to kiss her? Slowly they seemed to converge together, his breath on her face. Her pulse galloped as she anticipated his soft lips touching hers and her breath hitched as she closed her eyes. Then the crowd started to clap and Evan pulled away. Sara's disappointment was so acute it nearly brought tears to her eyes. But he'd made it very clear, over and over, he wasn't on dates. They were friends.

Friends. She didn't want to be friends anymore. She wanted him. But she knew his reasons and she couldn't put him in that awkward position. With what they had between them now, it was already going to hurt badly when he had to leave.

CHaPTer 12

Abby sat on the floor of the front room of her house, painting her toenails. She watched as Keira Knightly played Elizabeth Bennet in her favorite version of *Pride and Prejudice*. Where was her Mr. Darcy? She supposed Matthew Macfadyen looked more like Brandon than he did Will but neither man was like Mr. Darcy, really. Brandon wasn't uptight or conceited; he was opinionated and overconfident. Will. Well, if Abby were being honest, Will looked more like Mr. Wickham than he did Darcy. And sort of had some of the same traits as Mr. Wickham. That didn't necessarily make Abby feel better, but Mr. Wickham wasn't a real person.

Will was a real person. She was in a no man's land with Will. Since the party at Brandon's house, they'd been avoiding each other. She felt like a cartoon character with steam coming out of her ears when Evan had told her about the rating system the guys in the ward had for dating the girls in the ward. And it was only made worse because Will was standing right in the middle of all of it.

She shouldn't have been too surprised. He'd always had a taste for the kind of girls that would have rated high on that kind of scale. It offended her to no end that he would even include her, or allow anyone else to include her to be rated against that scale. She pulled his butt to the front yard and had some words with him. In true Will fashion, he'd batted those baby blues of his at her, told he had never, ever thought of her that way. It was all the other girls in the ward. That made her feel somewhat better but not really. She didn't want any of the girls to be rated like that. It was too harsh a system to measure up to.

Her phone pinged.

Are you home?

Yes, want to come over?

I'm outside

Why are you outside if ur not sure I'm home
front door's unlocked, just come in

Will was such a weirdo sometimes.

The front door opened and he strolled in.

"What are you doing?" he asked, looking around.

"What it looks like—painting my toenails and watching *Pride and Prejudice*."

"Haven't you watched this one like a million times?"

"Yes, and I still love it."

"Need some help?"

"You want to paint my toenails?"

"Sure, why not?"

"Okay," she said, giving him the you're-a-freaking-weirdo look.

"Can't I do a nice thing for my friend once in a while?"

"All right, sorry."

Will put her foot in his lap and proceeded to expertly paint her nails the pink she liked.

"So how's your week been going? Enjoying your summer off?" he asked.

"Yes. Sort of boring actually," she said, watching him work. She liked the feel of his hands on her feet. Gave her the tingles.

"I thought you were dating that guy, what's his name? The fluffy guy."

"His *name* is Brandon. And he isn't fluffy. And we're not officially dating. We've been on a few dates. And we have a date tonight."

"Oh," Will actually sounded disappointed.

"Why?"

"I was hoping we could go see a movie."

"Well, I would if I didn't have a date."

"Couldn't you, you know, fake a cough or something, ditch him and come with me?"

"No."

"Why?"

"Because I don't want to."

"You really like him?"

"Yes. But not as in 'love' like. As in, 'he's really nice to hang out with' like."

"Could have fooled me."

"Will, why do you even care?"

"I don't. I just wanted to know. You can do whatever you want—even if he is old."

Abby started laughing. "Twenty-five is hardly old."

"Older than us," he said defensively. "And too old for you."

"Oh?" Abby said, narrowing her eyes at Will. "And you're the one to determine that because . . .?"

"Because I'm your best friend and I have your best interest at heart."

"Is that what you call it? When you ditch me when you have a girlfriend and I don't hear from you for weeks and then suddenly you dump her or she dumps you and then I hear from you again?"

"But I always call you again."

Abby rolled her eyes. "You know if I didn't know any better, this conversation sounds an awful lot like jealousy, Will."

"No. Not jealousy. Concern for my friend."

"What is there to be concerned about?"

"I don't know," he said. "I don't know the guy very well. But what if he's just dating you to take advantage of you?"

"You're actually serious right now?"

"Yes."

"Well, let's see—he's been married before so he was responsible enough to get someone to marry him at least for a while. She wanted the divorce by the way, not him. He's got a son he loves very much and I'm sure he'd hate to go to jail on a cheap thrill so he'd never see his son again. He has a very good job at a computer company in Lehi, so you know he makes a good living. He wouldn't screw that up so he could take advantage of me because then he'd lose the house he bought *on his own*."

"You can't see how much you really like him."

"Okay, first of all, let's pretend for a second that you're right. Who cares? Why do you care? And secondly, what business is of yours who I date? I might make the odd comment about the girl you date but after that I just leave it alone. It's your life."

"Exactly. You make the odd comment. So am I. Here it is—he's too old for you. There it is. And we've already established that I don't care."

She stared at him in confusion and anger. Was he for real right now? This wasn't someone who didn't care. You didn't badger someone you didn't care about. Why wouldn't he admit it then?

"Okay, fine. I'll take your word for it. You don't care. If you're so concerned about me dating an older guy, then you date me. We're the same age."

It was Will's turn to roll his eyes. "That's not why I said something."

"Are you sure about that? Because that's what it sounded like. You don't like me dating older guys but yet no guy in the ward will date me because I'm not high enough on anyone's rating system to warrant getting asked out. At least if you dated me, then I would know you like me enough to be seen with me."

"I've never been embarrassed to be seen with you."

"I should hope not."

"We don't have to be girlfriend-boyfriend to hang out, Abby," Will said, finishing off her foot. "I enjoy our time together. It's nice to have someone rational to talk to when some of those girls are so freaking crazy."

Abby wanted to pull her hair out. She didn't want to push the issue, but she could have easily brought up that *that* was yet another reason he should consider dating her. They were already friends, already comfortable around each other. Why not take it to the next level? If he wasn't ashamed to be seen with her, then he wouldn't be ashamed to be seen hugging her or kissing her, right?

Abby shushed Will. It was the scene under the gazebo where Darcy and Elizabeth were soaking wet and Darcy was standing there like a moron trying to admit his love for Elizabeth. One day some guy would be standing in front of her, looking deeply into her eyes, desperately trying to tell her how much he adored and loved her. The thought came to her that if she waited for Will, she might be waiting forever. He had no incentive to want her. There were just too many distractions around. She sighed.

"Sometimes, I think life would be so much easier if romance was like in the movies. He comes straight up to you, looks you in the eyes and says, 'Darling, let's be together forever. Will you marry me?' And then you both run off into the sunset, happily ever after."

Will snorted. "Yeah, not gonna happen."

Abby pushed him. "Shut up. Let me have my dreams."

"Just because someone says the words doesn't mean they mean them."

"Now that is just a horrible thing to say, Will."

"It's true."

They sat and watched the rest of the movie together. Abby rested her head on Will's shoulder and just enjoyed his company. They really didn't have to say a whole lot when they were together. The only thing that marred the time they had left before she had to get ready for her date was her going over in her head what Will said. Just because you say fancy, lovely words doesn't mean you mean them. She knew he was right but it was a cynical way of looking at love because it meant you could never trust what someone was telling you. They could just be telling you what you want to hear. And that was worse than never being told at all.

CHaPTer 13

Sara put her backpack and violin case on her bed. She unzipped the case and pulled out her bow, tightened it, rosined it a little and pulled out the violin. She didn't need the sheet music anymore. She'd practiced the piece she and Evan were to play that morning so many times she had it memorized. She played it slowly to herself, thinking of all the times she'd watched him as his fingers worked the keys of the piano. One of the things she liked about him was how unaffected he was when he played. He didn't scrunch up his face dramatically or swing wildly back and forth. Rather, he hunched over the keyboard slightly in a way that was protective, almost intimate. His hands caressed the instrument so tenderly it was exciting to watch. He knew how to play so that only his feeling was put into the performance. That's what she liked. It's the way she liked to play—to channel her heart through her arms and fingers to the strings and through the sound that came out of the violin. Though she did like to close her eyes when she played. It helped her concentrate and pretend that she was the only one in the room, except lately Evan had joined her in that room and she played for him.

She felt how silly that was sometimes. If he were really there, she'd feel self-conscious, but the Evan of her imagination wasn't intimidating. He smiled at her and watched admiringly as she played. She wished he was that way in real life. He was very attentive when they were together. They had fun talking to each other and he made her laugh. But he also still maintained a distance from her. She'd tried to get the courage up a couple of times to ask him about it, but each time, she'd chicken out. Was it better to know? Or was it better to just keep things as they were and just hope that one day, he'd feel more comfortable being something more?

The doorbell rang and Sara went to answer it.

Evan stood there in his Sunday best. He looked handsome in the dark blue micro-pin-stripe and red tie.

"You look amazing," he said, looking at her.

Sara put a hand down to her dress. It was one of her favorite performance dresses—light pink with flutter sleeves. Nothing special she thought, but apparently Evan thought differently. She blushed.

"Thanks," she said. "You look nice, too."

"I thought if you didn't mind, I'd take you to church this morning so we can get set up," he said.

"That's a good idea," she said, smiling. "Let me go get my violin and tell Abby, and I'll be right back out."

She hurried back to the bedrooms and knocked on Abby's door.

"Abby, Evan's here to take me to church," Sara said excitedly when Abby opened the door. "I'll meet you there."

Abby's drowsy face smiled at her sister. "Have fun. I promise I won't be so late that I miss you guys' performance."

"Okay!" Sara said, hurrying back to her bedroom and putting away her violin.

She went back into the front room to find Evan standing there waiting for her. "Do you mind taking my violin and and I'll meet you out at your car?"

She couldn't help the way her heart fluttered a little as he took her instrument and she raced to get through the garage to meet him at his car. Maybe it was her. Maybe she was just being impatient with him. If he needed time to make sure he knew what he wanted, she could give him that. That way, he hadn't promised her anything and it would hurt less parting ways. She could respect that even if it was a little frustrating at times.

Of course, it wasn't like she had been exactly forthcoming with her feelings either. But he'd never asked her about them. And what if he had, or if he planned on it at some point? What would she be willing to say? She knew she'd have to tell him the truth. That she liked him more than any man she'd known in a while, and that was saying quite a bit. It had been nearly four years since she'd graduated from high school, and nearly six years since she'd seen Evan last. She'd had small crushes on a few others over the years but nothing close to the admiration and affection she felt for him.

They arrived at the church and set up and he sat next to her on the front row of the chapel.

Before the sacrament started, he leaned over to her and whispered, "Are you nervous?"

She looked over at him and breathed in the scrumptious scent of his spicy cologne. "A little."

"Just look at me, then. Don't look at the congregation. Either me or the bishop. I'd vote for me since I'm probably better looking than the bishop is."

Sara hid her mouth behind her hand and giggled. "Okay. Just you then."

She looked into his chocolate brown eyes, and adored he understood her so well. Sometimes she could almost sense there might be a feeling more than mere friendship from him. But she didn't dare hope too hard, because there were moments when he looked at her with such warmth in one minute, but in the next, his eyes would close off to her and she'd lose hope again.

When it was their turn and they were set up, she put the violin to her chin and looked over at him. He nodded at her and they played. It was beautiful and all too brief. She looked over at the bishop as she finished and he smiled and nodded a thank you at her.

She transferred back to the bench once she put her violin away and Evan came and sat down again next to her and reached over and squeezed her arm gently.

"We did a good job, I think," he whispered right into her ear. She couldn't help the huge smile and the slight shiver of warmth that ran up her arm at his touch.

They had several people approach them after the meeting was over, including Olivia and Will.

"That sounded great, Sara," Olivia said, a huge fake-looking smile on her face. "I mean I know Evan always sounds good, but I was really surprised at how good you are."

Sara tried to keep the smile on her face. "Thanks, Olivia."

"You shouldn't be so surprised," Abby said, coming up to them with Brandon in tow. "She and Evan practiced a lot together. Sara also practiced on her own, which was unnecessary because she has so much natural talent. She could have done that song in her sleep and still made it sound fantastic."

Abby's eyes narrowed on the other girl.

"You did sound wonderful," Evan said to Sara. Sara noticed Olivia giving her brother eye daggers as well when he said it. "And you're right, Abby, Olivia shouldn't be surprised. Sara's always been an extremely talented performer."

Sara could feel the blush spreading through her cheeks.

"Come on," Abby said, grabbing both Brandon and Will by the arms and dragging them down the hallway, forcing Olivia to follow them. "Let's get to class before we make Sara go beet red with all our compliments."

That only managed to make Sara blush harder.

"Don't be embarrassed," Evan said with a grin. "It's a good color on you."

"Stop," Sara said, covering her cheeks with her hands. "I feel like a cherry now."

"I have a surprise for you," he said, as he walked with her down the hallway.

"Really?" she said, smiling at him.

"The weather's been so nice lately and I feel like a well-played performance deserves a much-deserved celebration, so I've also arranged a small picnic for us after church. How does that sound?"

Sara opened her mouth to say something and for a moment she didn't know what to say, she was so pleased. When she recovered, she grinned and pushed his arm playfully.

"That sounds like a date," she said.

"Oh, um," he stuttered. It was his turn for his face to turn a little red at that point. "I guess it kind of does. Though it's not really, because it's Sunday. But if you'd like to go another day . . ."

"No, today is fine," she said. "The weather has been very nice."

"We'll ride together after church, I'll pick up the basket at my house, and then we'll go," he said, looking a bit troubled. "But just so you know, it's not a date."

"It's okay," Sara said. "I understand." Did he have to keep protesting it so hard?

"I'm sorry," he said. "I know you do. Just thought it sounded inappropriate for a Sunday. And things still need to be worked out--"

Olivia peeked her head out of the door of the Sunday School room, scowling at the both of them. "Are you guys coming? You are so slow."

As promised, he drove them to his house, picked up the basket and then drove towards the park where he picked a nice spot where they could sit under a tree and enjoy sandwiches, chips, sodas and cute bakery-made cupcakes.

As she expected, he avoided any topic that might lead to discussing what he meant when he said he needed to work things out. The only thing she could think of was maybe he was talking about school. He did say, when he first started to come to the ward, that he was only going to be there for the summer and that he hadn't decided where to go to school in the fall. Except why not talk about it? They'd already talked a million times about his unwillingness to decide. They'd never talked about what exactly he wanted to do. Maybe talking about that would help him make a plan of action that his parents could respect even if maybe it wasn't what they wanted for him exactly.

"I have had the best time hanging out with you this summer," he said as he lay back on the blanket, peeling the wrapper off his cupcake. "It's nice to talk to you. You know what you're talking about when you discuss music and things like that. My family thinks all that stuff is boring so I never really have anyone I can talk to about it."

"Well, I'm glad you feel you can talk to me," Sara said. "Sometimes I feel the same way as you about my family, though Abby tries her best to be supportive. She just doesn't find music, especially classical music, or art as interesting as I do. Evan, tell me the truth. With this new phase in your education, if you could do anything, earn any degree at all, what would you do? And I'm not talking about what your parents want you to do. What do you dream about?"

He looked at her for a moment as if deciding if he really wanted to tell her or not. He took a big bite of his cupcake.

"You're going to think I'm crazy," he said, after clearing his mouth. She shook her head and he looked away as he said, "I want to be Brandon Sanderson."

"What?" Sara asked. "You want to be Brandon Sanderson. What do you mean?"

"I want to do what he does. I want to teach college English. And when I'm not teaching, I want to write books."

"You do?" Sara asked, a big smile spreading across her face. "What kind of books?"

"I've got lots of ideas," Evan said, straightening up a little. "Mostly sci-fi and fantasy ones. I love to worldbuild. I love working with words. In some ways I wish I had gone to BYU so I could have taken his writing classes, but my parents thought it was a better overall education at Arizona State; plus, that's where my grandfather and father graduated from."

"I would love to read what you've written some time," Sara said.

"You would?" Evan looked at her surprised.

"Yes," Sara said. "I wouldn't have said it if I didn't mean it. I like speculative fiction too. I actually do quite a bit of fan art on my Deviant Art account when I'm not working on more traditional pieces."

She lowered her head to hide her blush. "I just didn't want to show you those because I didn't want you to think I was some weirdo drawing *Lord of the Rings* and *Labyrinth* pictures."

"Can I see?" he asked.

She pulled her phone out and brought up her Deviant Art account. She handed him her phone to look at.

"Wow," he said softly. "Are these done in oils?"

"No, that's done on a Wacom tablet and Photoshop. I learned how to use them from a classmate of mine, and from YouTube. So, self-taught mostly, but I used my colorwork knowledge from Art Theory classes, and there are all kinds of Photoshop virtual paint brushes that simulate the different textures you get from oil, acrylic and pastels that generate the different looks."

"I'm stunned, Sara," he said. "I really am."

She smiled at him. "So, I showed you my work, now you have to show me yours."

"I can't brag I'm as gifted as you are," he said, giving her back her phone.

"That's not fair. You are if you're as passionate about it as you sound—if you're half as good at writing as you are at playing the piano," she said.

"Okay, I promise to show you, since you showed me yours," he said. #For a brief moment after he'd sat up, it looked like he wanted to lean into Sara, he stared at her so intently. His face got suddenly sad. "I wish . . . I wish things were different. I wish I had made different choices than I have."

"You can tell me anything, Evan," Sara said, putting her hand over his. "If nothing else, I want to be your friend. I . . . I wish things were different, too . . . because of the way I feel about everything. But maybe that's too hard for you to hear."

"Sara," he said, squeezing her hand. "I really need to tell you something. Something about Arizona State while I was down there, so that you understand. I just hope you don't hate me after."

"Hate's a strong word," Sara said, still clinging to his hand. But something in the words he used had her shaking inside. Something he was going to tell her, she was not going to like. But for his sake, she was willing to hear whatever it was he needed to say. As much as she cared for him, she doubted that she could ever hate him. Disappointed, maybe. Sad, possibly. But not hate.

"When I was down at ASU, there was this—"

Evan's phone rang. "Dang it." He tried to ignore it and looked back up at her to start again but when it rang again, he answered it.

"Yes, Mom?" he said, his eyes pleading an apology to her. "What?"

Sara felt the fingers in his hand turn cold. "She did what? Why? What business was it of hers? Now is not a good time for this. I've already told her that. I can't talk about this right now. I'm on my way home."

He hung up his phone and threw it on the grass. He pulled his hand out of Sara's and stood up.

"I've got to go," he said flatly. "I'm sorry I have to cut our picnic short but something's come up at home and I've got to go take care of it."

"Okay, that's fine," Sara said, confused and worried. She got back in her wheelchair and helped Evan get the basket packed back up. Before he shut it all the way, he handed her the cupcake she hadn't eaten.

"You forgot this," he said, giving her a half-hearted smile. "It matches your dress."

"Thanks," she said, taking it from him. "We should do something this week. Want to come over for dinner again?"

"I don't know," he said. "I'll have to let you know. This week may not be the best."

She nodded, a sense of dread filling her insides.

"Let's get you home."

CHAPTER 14

Abby paced back and forth in the front room. Sara had come home last Sunday, went straight to her room and to bed. It was only the next day when she told Abby what had happened. Abby texted Will to see if he knew what was going on in the Farris house but he said he hadn't heard about anything unusual happening there that week.

The whole thing was odd. The following Sunday, neither Evan nor Olivia had shown up for church and, once again, Will pled ignorance of anything weird going on with the Farrises. Nor had Sara gotten one text, email, or phone call from Evan. Abby worried about her sister. Sara's normal energy was muted but she carried on like she always did, pretending like nothing was wrong when Abby knew better.

A knock came at the door. Brandon stood there. "You okay?"

"I'm not sure," Abby said. "Come in for a minute."

"Okay."

Brandon came in and sat down. Abby sat down next to him. His presence was comforting after the weird couple weeks they'd had.

"Have you heard anything from Evan?" Abby asked.

"No," Brandon said. "That's not terribly unusual. He doesn't text me that often."

"Would you mind trying to text him and see if he'll answer you."

"Why what's going on?"

"You know he wasn't at church last Sunday?"

He nodded.

"He's basically disappeared off the face of the planet. He took Sara out for a picnic the Sunday they played the song at church. He got a weird phone call, dropped her at home, and she hasn't heard from him since. I mean they usually text every day. But there's been nothing. She's been putting on a brave face for everyone but I know her. She's hurt. The least he could do is explain himself."

Concern was written all over Brandon's face. "Yeah, let me send that text now."

He typed out a message.

"I'm glad you said something," he said. "That is concerning. But then again this whole situation with him has been weird from the beginning."

"You're not kidding. He obviously really likes her. She feels the same but he won't call what they do 'dates?'" But they are. She was telling me that she's told him all about herself, which is great because people tend to talk over her. But when she asks about him and what his future looks like, he sidestepped every question. I mean I get that going to graduate school is a huge decision and you don't want to get trapped in a job you won't like, but he's so tight-lipped about everything."

"We'll help her figure it out," he said.

"We?" she said with a smirk.

"Yes, we," he said, taking her hand. "Two people who care a lot about her, right?"

"Yes," she said. She watched her hand in his. It felt good there and she realized it was the first time he had tried to get physical with her, even if it was small. She also realized that she liked it.

"I have something to ask you," he said.

"No, I won't marry you," she said, bringing her eyes back up to his.

Brandon's mouth hung open and then he started laughing. "Not the question I was going to ask but just for the record, that does sting a little to be rejected so completely."

"I just thought I'd put it out there for now," Abby said, smiling.

"For now, huh?"

She nodded.

"My company's summer party is coming up and I wondered if you would go with me? It's nothing fancy. They've rented out a pavilion at some park and there will be food and games and stuff like that."

"That sounds like fun," she said. "I'll go with you."

"Great," Brandon said. His smile spread from ear to ear. "Why don't we go find something to do while we're waiting to see if Evan returns my text?"

"What did you have in mind?"

"Did I see a little park down the road a bit?"

"I think so. I've never been down there."

"Let's go." He stood up and held his hand out to her. She took it and he helped her to her feet. Instead of letting her hand go, he kept it in his until he opened the door for her.

Abby felt a little thrill in her chest. He wanted to hold her hand, and she didn't mind it. She liked the way her hand felt in his. And holding hands didn't mean they were engaged or anything. It was just a nice gesture. Before they hit the sidewalk, she took his hand again and threaded her fingers through his. She smiled up at him. His eyes were really fantastic—a deep denim blue. She even liked how the skin around his eyes crinkled up when he smiled. It just highlighted the twinkle in his eyes when he did smile.

They didn't really say much as they walked. Her brain was going a million miles an hour trying to decide how she felt. One thing she was sure of. Walking next to Brandon felt good. There were no nerves, no worry she had to look and act a certain way. In a way it was like being with Will. She could just be herself around him. The biggest difference was that she knew Brandon wanted to be more than friends. Will never had.

"Penny for your thoughts," he said as they neared the park.

"Oh, just thinking about you," she said.

"Really?"

She nodded. "I've never met a guy like you. I don't feel like I have to impress you. I just get to be me."

"I'm glad you feel that way. I hope you want to show me the real you. I don't believe in being something I'm not just to get people to like me. Besides, once they found out I'm not really that way, they wouldn't like me anymore. I do like you, so, if you're being yourself, then I like the real you."

She looked at him. "I'm just me. I'm nothing fancy except my wicked sense of fashion. So what you see is what you get. And if you like that, then, well, good." She really wasn't sure what else to say to that.

They approached the little neighborhood park. It had the standard soccer/football field, and a playground set complete with swings. There weren't any kids, so they approached the playground.

"I used to love a good playground. My favorite was the swings. I used to get going so high, it would give my mom a heart attack."

"Want to swing? I'll push."

She grinned at him. "Sure. I feel a little silly though."

"Why?"

"Aren't I a little too old?"

"No. You're never too old to have fun."

She sat down on the seat and Brandon grabbed the swing at her waist. Having his hands and arms that close made her shiver a little. It made her imagine having his arms around her. She knew it would be easy to find out—all she'd have to do was step in close and he'd get the hint. Maybe. The question was—did she want to go from holding hands to hugging? Because, if you went there, the next step was kissing, and then, well, she wasn't ready to think beyond that yet.

She was having fun being swung back and forth when her phone rang. She sighed.

It was Will.

"What?"

"Geez, you're in a mood."

"I'm busy. Call me back later."

"You're on a date with him, aren't you?"

"None of your business. I'm hanging up on you."

"I need you to come take me—"

Abby clicked the End button and stuffed the phone back in her pocket.

"Did you just hang up on Will?"

"Yup."

At first, all Abby heard was something that sounded like Brandon was sneezing or choking. Then it became full blown laughter. Abby's phone started buzzing. She ignored it. She jumped off the swing and turned to face Brandon.

"You have to tell Sara. Or I will. She'll die laughing."

"It's funny but it isn't. I'm with you. I'd be rude to take his call when I'm with you."

He straightened back up and his mirth turned into a sweet smile. "Thanks."

"You're welcome. Will may think he's the center of the universe but he is wrong on occasion."

"I'd rather think he's wrong all the time." Brandon approached her and stood right in front of her. "But that's just my opinion."

"And as I've said before, you seem to have a lot of those."

"I do. Like I'm of the opinion that you're much more attractive when you stand up for yourself and the people you're with. Doormat isn't a very good look for you."

Abby's smile disappeared. "So glad you have so much confidence in me and my ability to handle my friends."

She folded her arms across her chest and walked back towards her house.

"Abby," Brandon said, jogging up to her. "Abby, wait." He held her elbow and turned her around.

"I didn't mean you're a doormat with everyone. You're not with me. You walking off mad at me proves that."

"But I am with Will. That's what you meant."

"Yes. But you just proved you don't have to be. You told him what you wanted and stuck by it. It didn't matter what he wanted, you were busy with me, so you didn't drop everything and help him. He's a big boy. He'll find a way to take care of himself. We all do."

"That sounds an awful lot like jealousy, Brandon."

"Let's just say, I don't understand why you let him steer you when you're more than capable of making your own decisions. And you already know what you want, so why let him distract you?"

"I'm not. I'm still doing everything I need to do to become who I want to be. And besides, who says you wouldn't do the same thing?"

"Because I think your goals and dreams are awesome. I'd want to help you achieve them, not pout because they take too much of your time."

Abby rested her chin on her chest, trying not to tear up. Will had never come out and said he didn't want her to achieve her goals. He never said he wouldn't support her in becoming a pharmacist. But he never really cared if she had studying to do or had class, and he never listened when she talked about her goals. He was more concerned with his paycheck every other week and how good he looked most of the time.

Brandon's arms wrapped around her back and pulled her into him. She rested her head on his chest. He had a woodsy smell like sanded pine. Being held by him was exactly like she thought it would be, and she didn't want him to let go. She wrapped her arms around him.

He was right, of course, and that was a hard thing. She didn't want to have to admit it. Not because she thought he'd hold it over her—but because, until she'd met him, there were things about Will that she just put up with or ignored. Brandon made her reconsider all those things because he was a lot of things Will wasn't—in every comparison, Brandon was better. It wasn't just about maturity—Brandon ran circles around Will in that vein, which was to be expected since he was older, had been married, and already had a child. He had a lot of qualities that Abby could respect. He was an active member, neither staunchly puritan nor apathetic. He had a simple testimony and he did the best he could, sort of like her dad. Course, her dad had gone a little crazy at first when he joined the Church but then he mellowed out as he got older. Brandon was like the mellow version of her dad. Will never took anything seriously, least of all church. He went to church every Sunday but she suspected that was because his friends were all there, including her.

Brandon pulled away, took her hand back in his, and headed back towards her house.

"The company party is this coming Saturday so I'll come pick you up at noon because things are going to get started around one p.m. Sound good?"

"Yup. I'm sort of excited to meet the people you work with."

"I'm excited for you to meet them. As much as I talk about you and Sara, they probably think I have a couple of imaginary friends."

Abby giggled.

"I'm very real, very flawed, and can be a terrible brat sometimes."

"But a beautiful brat who feels bad after she is. That's the big difference between a true brat and someone who just has a bad moment or two. True brats don't feel sorry for the way they acted."

"Are you referring to Olivia?"

"Maybe."

Abby laughed and leaned her head on his shoulder. "She is a true brat. I wonder how Evan puts up with her."

"Speaking of Evan . . ." Brandon pulled his phone out and checked it. He looked at Abby and shook his head. "I still haven't heard anything. I'll keep an eye on it. I may try one other time during the week, but I have no idea what is going on."

"I hope it's nothing bad, for Sara's sake. Maybe he finally decided on a graduate program and he doesn't want to have to tell her."

"From what I know about him, that doesn't sound right," Brandon said. "I don't think he'd be able to walk away from Sara without giving her some kind of explanation."

"I would have said so before too, but this ghosting of his is worrying."

Brandon nodded and they continued their walk back to the house, hand in hand.

CHaPTer 15

Abby and Brandon arrived at the park for his work party, and it looked like someone had dropped a carnival off. There were balloons and brightly colored tables with tons of catered food.

"This looks like it's going to be fun," Abby said as Brandon opened the car door for her.

"Yeah, sure does," he said. "What do you want to do first?"

"Let's just walk around a bit and see what there is and then decide."

"Smart plan."

She took his hand and laced her fingers with his. They got about twenty feet when a man pushing a baby stroller stopped in front of them.

"Brandon, hey!" he said. "I see you made it. Is this Abby?"

"It is," Brandon said with a big smile. "Abby, this is Gordon Montgomery. He's in Quality Control."

"Hi, Abby. It's nice to finally meet you," he said, shaking her hand. "This is my wife, Cassidy and our baby Katie."

Abby squatted down in front of the stroller to take a closer look at the little girl sitting there. She was wearing a pink gingham sun dress and had an explosion of downy blonde hair on her head.

"Hi, Katie," Abby said, reaching in and shaking the baby's hand. The little girl gave Abby a wide, mostly toothless smile—only two little pearls on the bottom. "She's so cute."

"Thanks," Cassidy said. "Are you two engaged?"

"Oh, no," Abby said. "We're just dating."

"You make an adorable couple."

"Honey," Gordon chided.

"I'm just saying."

"We'll see you guys around the party," Gordon said. Before they got too far, Gordon turned around and mouthed the word, "Sorry."

Brandon chuckled.

"So, I guess I can't touch any more babies or they'll think we're engaged," Abby said, shaking her head.

"Would that be so terrible?"

"No, but we've already had this conversation," Abby said. "I'm not ready."

"I understand. Neither am I."

"Then why did you ask?"

"Because I wanted to see what you would say."

"Well, that makes all kinds of sense."

"It does. If you had said yes, I might have gotten up on one of the picnic tables and announced to the whole company that we're engaged. That way there'd be no more questions about it."

"Yes, because that would solve everything."

"It'd solve some things."

She gave him a bland look, but she couldn't help but smile eventually anyway. She grabbed his hand and pulled him towards a booth with signup sheets set up.

"Hi," a friendly looking older lady said when they approached. "These are all the field games we're going to play today. Some are individual games but others are couple and group games. Each one has the prize for the winners listed at the top. Look it over and see if there are any you'd like to try for."

"Do you want to try any of these?" Brandon said skeptically, looking over the different games.

"I don't know," Abby said, her nose crinkling a little. "I don't need an Xbox or an overnight stay at the Hilton." She perused the other sheets until she gasped. She pointed at one of them. A hundred-dollar gift card to Ulta? "Brandon, can we do this one, please?"

"Which one?" he looked over her shoulder. "The three-legged race? A hundred-dollar Ulta gift card. Oh, I see. I can see all the colors of lipstick and eyeshadow dancing in your eyes."

"Yes! Please?"

He tried to give her a look like he was thinking about it, but she tugged on his arm and he broke out laughing. "All right, fine. You know I really suck at field games."

"I'm not the fastest runner ever, but that's not the point. It's about working together as a team. The one that does it the best is the one that usually wins. Or the one that can drag their partner across the grass fast enough."

He bent over and signed them up for the three-legged race. She clapped her hands together. "I hope we win. That would be so cool."

"How about we get some lunch first?" he said. He looked at the nice lady. "What time do the games start?"

"At about two thirty, so you've got about an hour to eat."

Once they got their food, they sat down at one of the pavilion tables. Abby caught him glancing over at her several times. The last time, she reached over and moved some of his hair off his forehead.

"I know we can do it. And I'll give you a bright pink lipstick kiss mark right on your cheek when I get the new MAC color I want."

"Is that a promise?" he said with a cheeky grin.

"Yes," she said. "Just for being willing to go along with it."

"Hey, bro!" a voice came from behind them. Someone came up behind Brandon and shoved him forward into the table.

"Bradley, you idiot," Brandon said, elbowing the guy in the ribs. "Meet my friend, Abby."

"*The* Abby?" the guy asked.

"Holy cow, does the whole company know who I am?" Abby asked, turning around to meet Brandon's friend.

"The CEO probably doesn't. But he's not in the office much," Bradley said. He was an amiable looking guy, tall and skinny with bright red hair and as many freckles as there were stars in the sky. "I'm Brad. Brandon and I are on the same team."

"Nice to meet you," Abby said, shaking his hand. She narrowed her eyes at Brandon. "Seriously, does everyone know about me?"

"I mention you from time to time," he said, shrugging. She looked over at Bradley who looked like he was about to laugh.

"Right," Abby said. It was flattering in a way. He liked her enough to talk about her. At the same time, it was a lot of pressure. There was a lot of expectation from these people about her and Brandon. If she ultimately decided they weren't right for each other, he'd have to spend a whole lot of time explaining to people they weren't seeing each other anymore. But for her part, she hoped he hadn't gotten his hopes up too high.

She realized she liked him, and it was definitely more than a friend like—probably somewhere along the lines of serious crush like. If Will wasn't in the picture, she might even consider becoming exclusive with him. But then again, maybe not. It was like when she looked at Brandon, she saw a lot of potential in him. Like if boys had a dating-and-marriage potential resume, his would be a very nice one. He had a lot to offer—he was employed in a field where he would be able to grow, just like hers. He had a child already and seemed open to the idea of more eventually. He wasn't against the idea of marriage. He went to church every Sunday and seemed to take his church duties seriously. He already owned his own home and car. Even though he'd been married before, he and his ex seemed to be on decent terms. On paper there wasn't much about him not to like.

But sometimes, his opinions—and his tendency to share them whether they were wanted or not—was annoying. His ability to be right in any given circumstance was especially annoying to Abby. And his disdain of Will grated on her nerves. Couldn't he just leave Will alone? Why couldn't he just mind his own business instead of taking every opportunity to point out Will's shortcomings? She, more than anyone in the ward, knew what those were and, like everyone else, she accepted them as part of who he was.

But it was getting harder to ignore that when Brandon looked at her, there was something in his eyes that drew her in. Sometimes at church, or when he was over at her house, she'd catch herself staring at his mouth and thinking what it would be like to kiss him.

Ever since the swings, he'd often take her hand; she'd come to expect it if he was nearby. He didn't hug her very often, but when he did, that's what she liked best—being encircled by his surprisingly muscular arms. He probably didn't do it often because they didn't get very much alone time. He'd been busy at work and sometimes had late nights, or she'd be busy with Will and miss her chance to see Brandon.

Today, though, she felt he'd take the chance because everyone around them expected it and he felt comfortable here. He didn't feel the need to hide his feelings for her. And for her part, she liked the feeling of being open and comfortable with him too.

The booth lady got up on a ladder and announced with a big megaphone, "All those that have signed up for field games, please come back to the booth to get your numbers, then line up at your individual race lines."

"I guess that's our queue," Abby said, standing up. "It was nice meeting you, Brad."

"Same," he said, holding up a hand. "Maybe we'll see you around."

"Maybe," she said. She pulled Brandon up and walked over with him to the booth.

A new lady handed them their numbers and said, "Just pin these on each other's backs, then tie this length of rope around your inside legs and wait your turn," the event helper said.

"You ready for this?" Abby asked, as she pinned the large number on Brandon's t-shirt.

"I was born ready," he said in a gruff voice.

Abby giggled. "Good. We're going to need all the help we can get."

"If we win, do I get to pick a fingernail polish for you?" he asked, turning around to pin her number on her back.

"I think that's a fair request, even though you are getting the big pink kiss mark on your cheek."

"It just gives me an excuse to paint your nails," Brandon said when she turned around.

"Deal," she said, tapping him on the chest with the rope.

They lined up on the field and Brandon tied the rope around their ankles.

"Now, strategy meeting," he said. "Let's start with the tied legs and then the outside legs. Will counting help?"

"Probably. I've heard it also helps to hang onto your partner to stabilize the tied legs and you'll be less likely to trip." She moved in to stand next to Brandon, hip to hip. She put her arm around his shoulder. "You should probably put your arm around my waist."

"If I didn't know better, I'd say you're just looking for a reason for me to hold you."

"That wouldn't be the worst thing that could happen," she said, smiling up at him.

"Abby, you are so much fun to hang out with," he said, his eyes soft. "It's such a nice bonus that you're absolutely beautiful too."

Abby's cheeks burned and she looked down at her feet. "Thanks. I like hanging out with you too."

"You do?"

"I haven't said before?"

He shook his head.

Abby opened her mouth. "I'm sorry. I should have said something. I do. I have a lot of fun when I'm with you."

His smile split his face.

"Okay, next up—the three-legged race. On your marks . . . Get set . . . GO!"

They almost fell on their faces. Abby tried to lead with her dominant leg and forgot that she was supposed to start with the tied leg first. Brandon caught her as she screamed but managed to keep her up right.

"Okay, ready? One . . . Two . . . One . . . .Two . . ." Once they got a good rhythm going, they caught up to the rest of the racers. Since they were both slightly taller than the rest of the them, they easily overtook the other couples struggling to keep in sync with their partners.

"One . . . Two . . . One . . . Two . . .Keep going! We can do it!" Brandon shouted. They made it across the finish line first but Abby's foot caught the edge of the grass, sending them both to the ground in a pile.

Laughing, Abby hugged Brandon's chest.

"We did it!" she said "You okay?"

He wiped some tears from his eyes. "Yes," he chuckled. "Not quite the grand finish I envisioned."

"But the important part is, we won!" she exclaimed as she untied the rope from their ankles.

He managed to get back on his feet, and pulled her up to him. Instead of just taking her hand, his hand went around her waist again, and Abby didn't mind a bit.

Brandon looked around the park as Abby picked up her gift certificate. "It's getting kind of hot. You want to go investigate that path over there? Try out the shade of the trees."

"Sounds great. Lead on."

Hand in hand they wandered down the walking path under the canopy of trees.

"Abby," Brandon said, pulling her hand and stopping her.

She turned to look at him.

"I've had a lot of fun today. Thanks for coming with me."

"I have, too. I liked meeting some of the people you work with. And you can't beat a free lunch, right?"

He chuckled. He laced his fingers between hers and drew her nearer. "I don't believe in being coy or dishonest about how I feel. I think you've known for a while how much I like you."

She looked into his mountain-lake blue eyes and nodded.

"I'm not going to ask you to feel the same way I do," he said, stepping in closer so that his face was mere inches from hers. "But I do want you to know how I feel."

Abby's heart started beating faster. She'd thought when she got to this point with a guy—especially Brandon—she'd feel uncomfortable or awkward, but standing here with him felt normal, intimate. That generous mouth of his was so close she could almost feel the lips sweep against hers as he talked causing her stomach to flit around.

"You're one of the coolest, most amazing women I've met in a long time. I'd feel lucky if I was able to win your heart, but I know you have other . . . priorities you have to think about right now. I just want you to think about it. Think about me."

With his free hand, he reached up and swept his fingers across her cheek as he tucked a lock of hair behind her ear. The touch caused little spurts of fire to shoot through her, hitching her breath. When his hand went to her face, she closed her eyes and leaned in as he kissed her lips.

The blood roared in her ears and she grabbed onto his shoulder for support. He took his time, slowly kissing every part of her mouth as he wrapped the hand that had been on her face around her waist again. She was glad of the support because her knees felt weak enough to drop her. She wasn't able to get enough oxygen, her pulse was racing so fast.

She finally pulled away so she could take an adequate breath and had to blink a few times to get herself under control.

"I . . . Brandon, I . . ." she stumbled. She had no idea what to say. "I will think about it. I've never been kissed like that before."

He hugged her and she put her head on his shoulder. He wrapped his arms around her and just held her. If this was what being with him meant, then he was a very good choice. But what was she thinking? Being with him? She had school coming up. She had plans that didn't include marriage and children yet, and he was at an age where that's what he would want. The thought of his expectations for her created icicles in her stomach.

She looked up at him again. Putting both her hands on his face, she pulled his face down and kissed him again. It was easy to forget about the stuff that made her confused or scared when he made her feel like this—his soft lips against hers and his arms around her waist, holding her close to him.

What did she want? Did she want him? Right now, she did. He was an amazing kisser. But would she feel the same way tonight? Tomorrow? Later in the week? Time would tell. For now, she just let herself melt into him. She tried very hard not to think of Will and all the times *he* could have done this with her but had spurned her.

Brandon wanted her, and right now, she wanted him, too.

CHAPTER 16

Abby's emotions were all over the place. It had been four days since the outing at the park. Four days since the kiss. Brandon texted her everyday, sat with her at church and came over to her house whenever he could. He seemed to be stepping carefully with her, taking her lead in everything. The problem was after the magic of that afternoon had gone, she couldn't decide what she wanted. She hadn't even told Sara about kissing him. Not because she was ashamed or regretful, but because her feelings about everything were a knotted mess. She still couldn't look at Brandon without remembering their kisses at the party—and her heart would react each time. She could see he felt the same.

The biggest knot in the yarn of her feelings was Will. And Will had gone AWOL. He had only messaged her in the past two weeks if she had reached out to him first. He'd refused all invitations to go anywhere with her. She'd only seen him once—at last week's activity.

Abby's phone rang in her hand. She jumped to answer it, but paused when she saw it was Will.

She answered with a sarcastic, "Well, now I feel worthy again. What did I do to deserve your attention?"

"Hey now," he said. "I've missed hanging out with you. Want to go to the mall and see what's new for fall?"

"No, not particularly," she said.

"Come on," he said. "You don't have anything better to do, and I want to hang out."

"Why? Where's Olivia?" Abby asked.

"She's somewhere," Will said.

"Where?" Abby insisted.

"She's getting her hair done, okay?"

Abby snorted in disgust. "You suck. I am not going to sit on the back burner for you just because you get lonely. I have better things and better people to occupy my time."

"Hey, I'm offering you a legitimate reason to come hang out with me," he said.

"Yeah, doing something you want to do. Did you even think about whether it was something I wanted to do?" she asked. "You know what? I'm going to call Brandon and see if he wants to go do something fun. He cares if I have fun or not."

"Go for it, then," Will said. "Date Fluffy. See if I care. I'm way funner than he is and you know it. At least I'm upfront and honest with you about our friendship. I don't expect you to put out eventually."

"What is that even supposed to mean, Will?"

"It means what it means," Will said. "It's what all guys expect of the girls they date."

"You're gross," Abby said. "Go sit on Olivia's lap while she gets her hair done. Maybe she'll pat your head and give you a doggy treat for being a good boy."

She hung up on him. Not once had Brandon made her feel uncomfortable or pressured, let alone act like he expected that from her. Will was just trying to get under her skin. Problem was, it was working.

Abby's cell beeped a few minutes later. Brandon.

Need a ride to the activity?

I guess so. I'm in no condition to drive
I have murder on the mind

Let me guess. Will.

Just come and get me. I'll be outside.

She pulled on the high heels she'd been wearing and walked out the front door. She shut it behind her a little harder than she needed to and threw herself down on the top step. She took in deep breaths to calm herself while she waited for Brandon. She stood up when she saw him driving down the street and got in the moment he pulled up.

"Are you—"

"Just drive," she said testily.

"Yes, ma'am," he said. "So, what happened?"

"Will is being his stupid self, as usual. Thought I wanted to spend hours following him around the mall while he shopped. Just for the pleasure of his company. Just because he's lonely and bored."

"I still don't get why you let him get to you like that. Why do you let him treat you like that?"

"Treat me like what?"

"Like you're an idiot and you'll just go along with whatever he says and does just because he says it and wants to do it?"

"I didn't though," Abby said.

"Yes, but for some reason he still thinks he can," Brandon said. "All the time. Why don't you make it clear to him you won't?"

"I have been, Brandon," she said, hurt. "And, excuse me, but I don't think my friendship with Will is any of your business."

"Probably not," Brandon said. "But it astounds me that a smart, beautiful woman allows herself to be treated like a toddler just because he's insecure."

Abby opened her mouth to say something, but she couldn't think of a rebuttal. At least nothing intelligent enough to come back with, and certainly nothing that would convince

Brandon she was doing exactly what he was telling her to—because Will was still doing it. That only made Abby more mad.

"Well, I'm so glad you're here to point these things out to me," she said, glaring at him. Brandon pulled up to the sidewalk in the church parking lot. She threw the door open. "Next time, I'll make sure to ask your opinion when I need to register my car or sign up for classes—because I'm such an idiot."

"Abby," Brandon said. "You know that's not what I meant."

"Then keep your nose out—" Abby had turned her head to look back at him before stepping up onto the curb of the sidewalk. She felt her ankle twist as her high heeled shoes missed the flat edge of the concrete. She screamed as she found herself falling backwards onto the asphalt.

"Ow!" she cried, reaching towards her ankle.

"Abby, are you okay?" Brandon came rushing around to her side of the car and knelt down next to her.

Tears flooded down her cheeks as she watched as her ankle grow right before her eyes, turning black and purple. "Oh, no!"

"Oh, no, is right," he said, putting an arm around her back to support her. A few others joined them to find out what had happened.

"Open the door for me, will you?" Brandon asked one of the guys standing there. He held her hand as he helped her up onto her good leg. With a gentleness she'd never felt from him before, he guided her back into the passenger seat and plugged her seatbelt back in.

"What are you doing?" she asked.

He looked at her with a grin, wiping away some of the tears from her face. "I'm taking you to the emergency room. Looks like, at best, you sprained your ankle badly; and, at worst, you broke it."

"Oh," she said, stunned. "Thanks."

He chuckled and shook his head. "Let's go."

He drove carefully, but she hissed every time he went over a bump too fast. She grabbed his hand as they neared the hospital. He held onto her tightly and hurried as fast as he could.

They found themselves in a small room at Riverton Hospital waiting for the nurse to come and do an evaluation. Abby hadn't been able to let go of Brandon's hand, even though several times it would have made getting registered and into the room a lot easier. She only let go when they put her up on the gurney inside the room.

"Brandon," she said in a small voice.

He looked over at her.

"I hate needles."

"Okay, if they put in an IV in, just look at me while they do it, okay?"

She nodded quickly. Tears streaked down her face.

The nurse pulled back the door. "What did you do?"

"I fell off the sidewalk and twisted my ankle," Abby said as the nurse gently touched the bruised and puffy ankle. Abby sucked in a breath.

"Hmm, looks broken but we'll get some X-rays to see how bad it is," she said. "In the meantime, let's get you some pain meds. Sound okay?"

Abby nodded again.

"I'll be right back with the IV and the meds."

She laid her head back on the gurney and turned her head away from Brandon. She hated that he had to see her like this but it made her feel better to have him sitting there and that they let him sit in with her at all. She guessed they assumed he was her boyfriend or husband or something.

"You doing okay?" he said, rubbing her arm. "Do you need anything?"

"No, I need to text Sara though."

She pulled the phone out of her pocket and sent her sister a quick message.

At the Riverton ER, broke my ankle, Brandon's here, text Will for me

She put the phone away and looked over at him.

"Brandon, I'm sorry I was being a brat earlier. I shouldn't have gotten angry with you. It wasn't your fault and you were just telling me the truth."

"Apology accepted, Abby," he said. "I won't say anything more about it tonight. It's not important. Getting your ankle fixed is. Let's just concentrate on that."

"Okay," she said, smiling at him. "I'm glad you're here."

"I'm glad I could be helpful," he said, smiling back.

The nurse came back into the room with her IV tray and Abby tensed. Brandon stood behind the gurney and took her other hand in his.

"So, did you get registered for all your classes for fall semester?" he said, looking down at what the nurse was doing. "Abby, look here up at me."

Abby looked up at him. "Um, yes. I've got Biology, Communications, Math. This shouldn't be too hard of a semester."

She hissed in a breath as she felt the pinch from the needle going into her arm.

"Doing good, Abby," the nurse said. "Almost done."

"Abby, what about dinner?" Brandon asked. "What did you have for dinner?"

"A Hostess cherry pie," Abby said looking back up at him.

"Really?" he said, laughing. "That's it?"

Abby started laughing too. "Yeah. That's all I could find in the fridge. I forgot to go to the grocery store the other day."

"No wonder you were raging so hard," he said, wiping laugh tears from his eyes. "You were on a sugar high."

"And now you'll be on a little painkiller high," the nurse said as she pushed the medicine from a syringe into Abby's IV. "Someone will be by soon to x-ray that ankle and then the doctor will be in to tell you the next step. Call if you need anything."

Sooner than she thought possible, Abby felt cozy and sleepy and the pain was nearly gone. She looked up at Brandon and smiled. He was so good to her.

"Feeling better?" Brandon asked.

"Yes," she said drowsily. "I'm so tired."

"Then go to sleep. I'll wake you if Sara shows up."

CHAPTER 17

Abby still felt so tired as they pulled up to her house and Brandon helped her out of the car. The boot was unwieldy, and the crutches weren't any better.

"Put your arm over my shoulder and I'll help you up the stairs," he said. "I'm not going to have you fall over asleep on these crutches. Sara pulled her car into the garage and hurried to get into the house and unlock the door for them.

Brandon put his arm around Abby's waist and slowly helped her up the stairs, then onto the front room couch while Sara got her pillow and blanket off the bed. Just as she was getting comfortable a soft tap came at the door.

"Who could that be?" Sara said to Brandon.

When she answered the door, Will stood there. "Sorry, I didn't get your text until just barely."

"I sent it three hours ago," Sara said, frowning.

"I was busy," he said, shrugging. He came up to Abby and knelt down next to her. "How are you feeling? How's your ankle?"

"Broken, and I feel like crap," she said. "I have to take these pain meds even during the night and until I have my appointment with the orthopedist."

Brandon rubbed his beard. "I wish I could stay longer but I have to get up for work tomorrow."

"Don't worry about it," Will said. "I don't have work, so I'll stay and make sure she gets her meds."

"Are you sure?" Sara asked. "That means you'll have to get up in the middle of the night to make sure she gets it on time or the pain will get worse."

"I'm not twelve," Will said defensively. "I can put an alarm on my phone to wake me up. Both of you go to bed, and I'll take care of it."

Sara looked like she wanted to protest but she also looked exhausted. "Fine. Let me get you a pillow and blanket and you can either sleep on the floor or on Abby's bed. Goodnight, Brandon. Thank you for all your help."

Brandon went over to Abby and took her hand. "I really wish I could stay. I'll come by tomorrow after work to check on you."

Abby smiled at him. "Okay, that sounds good. I'll see you tomorrow."

Brandon reached down and placed a short, soft kiss on her mouth. He turned and left without saying goodbye to Will.

Abby heard Will murmur the word "Jerk."

"How are you doing?" he asked her as soon as the door was shut. "Are you doing okay?"

"No, Will," Abby said, looking at him. "My ankle is the size of a cantaloupe and it hurts. The doctor says I'll be lucky if I don't need surgery on it."

"Man," Will said, pushing his hand through his hair. "What were you doing?"

"Yelling at Brandon," Abby said.

Will started to snicker.

"Shut up," she said. "It's not funny. I should have been paying attention to where I was walking."

"All right," he said, taking her hand. "I'm just sorry it took me so long to get here."

"Yeah, well, Brandon was here. He was a total sweetheart the whole time," she said, sighing. "He held my hand the whole time they were putting the IV in and made sure I got anything I needed until we came home."

There was silence between them while Sara came back into the room with the pillow and blanket for Will. Will waited for Sara to go to bed before turning back to Abby.

"So, what—are you in love with Brandon now or something?" Will asked.

"I don't know what I am, Will," Abby said. "All I know is I'm happy when I'm around him and he puts me first when I'm with him."

"Are you exclusive?" he asked.

"No," Abby said. "I haven't decided if I want to take that step yet or not."

"Why?"

"Because his life's too complicated for me to say I want to be his girlfriend. He's in a different stage in life. He has a son. And I still have things I want to do before I get married and start a family."

"You're overthinking it," he said. "He's too old for you and you shouldn't be dating him. End of story."

Abby narrowed her eyes at Will. "It's not that simple."

"I don't see what's hard about it," Will said.

"You wouldn't understand. Brandon actually cares about me as a person. He makes sure I'm happy and taken care of. He wants to hang out with me purely to have fun."

"What about me?"

"What about you?"

"Abby, I've missed you," he said.

Abby glanced over at him. "You don't have to say stuff like that just to make me feel better. I know you've been busy with Olivia."

Will shook his head. "No, I'm serious. Olivia's fine to hang out with but she isn't fun like you are."

Abby's mouth dropped open. "I . . . I miss hanging out with you, too, Will."

"I wasn't so sure," Will said, sitting down on the floor but not letting go of Abby's hand. With his other hand he started to pet the skin where the IV had been. "You've been giving me the silent treatment lately. And it wasn't until then that I realized how much I missed being with you."

"Will. I didn't think you wanted me to contact you. You were always with Olivia and I didn't want to get you in trouble with her, so I just stopped."

"You're not wrong. She wasn't exactly thrilled when I'd get texts from you," Will said. "It was like she was jealous or something. Why would she need to be jealous when I was with her all the time? That got kind of annoying after a while. It's not like you were trying to steal me from her or anything. And then I realized how you and I would just hang out. You didn't need me to do stuff, not really. It's always easy between us."

Will sat back up on his knees so he could look her in the face. "Do you know what I mean?"

"What are you trying to say, Will?" she said. Her head still seemed a little foggy and she wasn't sure if this was a dream or if she really was laying here on her couch having Will say things that he would have never hinted at before.

"I'm saying I miss you, Abby," he said. "All that time with Brandon and at school and I hardly ever get to see you or talk to you anymore."

His face loomed closer to hers.

"Will, you're dating Olivia," Abby said. Confusion washed over her.

"So?" Will said. "It's not like I'm married to her. And I've known you a lot longer than her. So why shouldn't I worry about you or wonder what you're up to?"

"Because you've never worried about any of that before," Abby said. She almost felt mad about it. He never really acted like he cared unless it affected him directly somehow.

She looked Will directly in his light blue eyes. They looked so sincere, and he was too close. Was he going to try and kiss her?

She put her hand on his chest and pushed him back. "I need to get some sleep. My head is a mess and my ankle is really sore." She hated that her hand trembled a bit.

"Okay," he said, softly. "I'll wake you up in a few hours for your next dose." He placed his hand over hers and held it against his heart. "Get some rest. I'll be right here."

Abby pulled her hand away from him and turned herself away, trying to get as comfortable as she could on the couch. The thoughts in her brain swirled dizzyingly around so that she couldn't make sense of what Will was doing. Suddenly he was acting all lovey dovey. But he was dating Olivia. And she was dating Brandon. Brandon had been so supportive and sweet the whole time she was in the ER. Brandon only ever seemed to be honest and upfront with her about everything. Will liked to sidestep the truth when he didn't want to tell it. Will had never before wanted to date her. He always went for girls like Olivia—beautiful, but vain and high-maintenance.

She fell asleep still not sure what was going on or why.

Sunlight sparkled through the front room curtains. Abby turned over on the couch and found Will lying on the floor next to the couch asleep. His hair was adorably disheveled and she reached down and softly moved the hair from out of his face. He stirred and then opened his eyes to look up at her and smiled. It took her breath away.

"Good morning," he said, stretching. "How are you feeling?"

"Sore still," she said. "But I think I'll be okay."

He sat up and leaned against the couch where she leaned on her elbow. "Need another dose of pain meds? It's almost time."

Abby smiled back at him. "I can wait. Thanks for staying the night."

"You're welcome," he said. "I was glad to do it for a girl I care so much about."

Abby didn't know what to say. She'd almost forgotten the weird conversation they'd had the night before.

"I was doing some thinking last night while you were sleeping," he said. He looked down as he played with the edge of his t-shirt. "I wanted to apologize for being a jerk lately."

"Wait a minute," Abby said, putting her hand out in front of his face. "Let me get my phone. I need to record this moment. Will is apologizing for something?"

"Yeah, yeah. Don't get too excited," he said, grimacing at her. "I'm serious. I haven't been very nice to you lately. And when you stopped contacting me, I was mad at first but now I can understand why. I've been a jerk, and you don't deserve that. You've been my best friend all these years and that's why I've missed you."

Abby watched his face. There wasn't any sign of joking or teasing in his face. He really did look absolutely serious about what he was saying. Abby could feel tears threatening behind her eyes, but she blinked them back quickly. There was something about all this that just didn't sound right but nothing about what he was saying and the way he said it came across that way.

He seemed to pause for a moment before he finally looked directly at her. "I don't want you to hate me."

"I don't hate you."

"You might when I say the next thing I'm about to say," he said. He searched her face. "I want to give us a try."

If Abby hadn't already been lying down, she would have fallen over. She did fall back against the couch, though. Her heart started to beat out of her chest.

"That's not funny, Will," Abby whispered. The tears she'd been fighting started to build up at the sides of her eyes.

He got back up on his knees. "I'm not joking. Abby. I wasn't kidding when I said I missed you. I kept thinking you'd call me or text me and then when you wouldn't it was like someone was pulling on my chest. It wasn't even something that Olivia could make feel better."

He reached up and wiped one of the tears that had slid down her face. "Will you? Will you give us a try?"

Abby couldn't answer him. Her brain was too confused. His face was so beautiful, as was his smile. She felt trapped by his blue eyes as he stared into hers. The heat from his hand on her face froze her in place. She put her hand over his on her face, and he leaned over and kissed her on the lips. She gasped but leaned into it. It was everything she'd ever imagined it would feel like, from the softness of his lips to the way he pressed them against hers. He had just pulled away and put his forehead against hers when Abby heard an "Oh!" come from the hallway that led to the bedrooms. She looked over and saw Sara sitting there.

"Um, I just came in to tell you I was planning on staying home from school today to take care of you," she said, looking from Abby to Will warily. "But I guess I won't?"

"Yeah, go to school, Sara," Will said. "I don't have to work. I'll take care of Abby today."

"Will, can I talk to my sister for a sec?" Sara asked.

"Yeah, I have to go to the bathroom anyway," he said, getting up. "I'll be right back."

Abby had a hard time looking Sara in the eye when Will disappeared into the bathroom.

Sara hurried over to her. "What are you doing? What is going on? I thought you were dating Brandon?"

"Sara, Will wants to date me," Abby said. She felt like she couldn't breathe saying it. "He just told me. He's missed me."

"But what about Brandon?" Sara said, wringing her hands.

"What about him?" Abby said.

"Abby."

"I mean, it's not like we're exclusive or anything," Abby said, looking away from her sister.

"Are you going to tell him?"

"Of course. I'm not a jerk like that. He deserves to know."

Sara put her head in her hand. "Okay. I just— You know what? Never mind. It's none of my business. You date whomever you want."

"Sara, please?" Abby pleaded. "You understand, right?"

"Yes, Abs, I do," Sara said. "I understand all too well. I don't happen to agree, but that doesn't mean anything if Will is who you want."

"I know you and Brandon are friends," Abby said. "And Brandon is a good guy but I just have to know if Will—"

"Abby, you don't have to explain to me," Sara said. "I understand. Just please contact him soon. Don't leave him hanging. I guess I'll go to school, then, if you'll have Will here. Unless you don't want me to."

"No, go," Abby said. "I'll be fine. We'll be fine."

Sara took one last worried look at her sister and then turned back to her room to get her stuff.

Before she left, Sara turned to Will. "Take good care of her, Will. I'll be back at my regular time, Abby."

"Don't worry about Abby, Sara. She'll be just fine with m—" Sara shut the garage door on him before he could finish his sentence.

"Well, I guess she wasn't happy about it."

"She's fine. She's just friends with Brandon now and she's worried."

"Brandon's a big boy. He'll be fine."

"I hope so."

CHAPTER 18

A knock came at the door later in the day.

"Come in. It's unlocked!" Abby yelled.

Brandon opened the door with a small bouquet of flowers in his hand and a smile on his face. Abby's resolve faltered a little when she saw him.

"Hey," he said. "Comfortable? Do you need anything?"

"I'm fine. Come on in," Abby said, trying to plaster a smile on her face. "There's a glass in the dishwasher you can put those in. I need to talk to you for a moment when you come back."

"Okay," Brandon said, his smile now abating a bit at her vague statement.

He pulled up a dining room chair and sat down next to her. "So, were you able to get some rest today?"

"Pretty much. I've been keeping on top of my pain meds so I've been sleeping a lot today."

"Good. I didn't send you any texts today because I figured that's what you'd be doing."

"So, um, Brandon, I wanted to talk to you about something," Abby said, twisting the edge of her blanket in her fingers. "I wanted to let you know that I really appreciated everything you did for me yesterday. That was really sweet of you."

Brandon sat up straighter in his chair. "Why does it sound like there's a *but* in there?"

"There is," Abby said, glancing at him. "Last night after you dropped me off, Will and I had a chance to talk. He's missed me these last few weeks and I admit I've missed him, too. We've been friends for a long time and I'd hoped there could be more, but he'd always assured me there couldn't be . . . until last night."

Brandon's face grew stony.

"As much as I really like you, I've always liked Will more. You know that. And I know I sound like a total jerk, but I figured you'd want me to be honest with you rather than lie just to make you feel better."

"So you've agreed to start dating him, is that it?"

"Yes."

Brandon sat there silent for a minute. Then he shook his head. "I just don't get it. You're a smart, beautiful, confident woman and yet you insist on throwing yourself at such a moron. And not just a moron, but one that treats you like absolute garbage when it suits him. And then, even more shocking is tht you *let him*!" His voice had been slowly increasing in volume until he'd spoken in just below a yell.

"He is not a moron," Abby said. "He may not be the smartest guy on the planet but he's fun and funny and he knows me better than anyone except Sara. I don't require him to be super smart in order to find value in him. I never did. #Just because you're a smart guy doesn't mean that I have to like you better."

"I'm not saying that," Brandon said. "I'm saying I thought you valued *yourself* better. Why date someone who puts you second; who constantly turned away from you to date someone else; who acted like you were only there for his convenience? If you don't like me enough to keep dating me, fine. I'll stop asking you. But don't mistake my anger with Will for jealousy. Just about any other guy in the ward is a better guy for you than him."

"I think it's time you leave," Abby said. "You're being really unfair to a person I happen to care about. You barely know him. You barely know *me*. You just assume you know—you've done that from the beginning—and you don't know *anything*. I think you get my message: I want to date Will. That doesn't mean I'm not grateful for yesterday, but you're being so rude right now, and I don't want to say something I'll regret."

"Fine," Brandon said, standing up. "Me, either. I care about you, Abby. I hope one day you understand how much. I'm leaving like you want me to. I won't stand around and watch you date Will—because I think you'll regret that choice in the end."

He stormed out the door and slammed it shut.

Abby put her face in her hands and let out a shuddering breath. She sat there like that for a moment trying not to cry. Her brain was telling her she'd made the right decision but her heart didn't agree. It hurt to see him so angry, and what he'd said had stabbed her through. He wasn't worried about himself. Not really. He was talking about her. He thought she was smart, beautiful, confident—and that wasn't the first time he'd called her those things. Will never said any of that to her, but she'd never expected him to. She'd just assumed he thought it.

The front door opened up a few minutes later and Will walked through.

"Am I too early?" he said, coming through with two bags of fast food in his hands. Will occupied the chair that Brandon had abandoned. She watched him as he pulled out her dinner and placed it in front of her.

"No, you're right on time. Brandon just left."

"Great. Now we can eat in peace. I got your favorite—the crispy chicken sandwich."

"Oh. I actually like the grilled better, but it's not a big deal. I'm still hungry."

"Is he gone for good?"

"Well, gone for now," Abby said.

"What?" Will turned and looked at her.

"He might be back," Abby said, digging through her dinner bag. "He and Sara have gotten to be good friends and it's not like I can tell her who she can hang out with."

"But does he have to come here? She couldn't go to his house or something?"

"Will," Abby said, pulling on his sleeve. "She lives here too. It's not like he'd be able to talk me back into going out with him. Is that what you're afraid of?"

"Why would I worry about that?" Will said, eyebrows pinched together. "He's only in love with you."

Abby rolled her eyes, though the idea of that did give her a thrill to her stomach. She pushed it back though. She was in love with Will, not Brandon. She finally had a chance to be with Will and she was not going to throw it away just because there was a little part of her that had a crush on Brandon.

He turned his back to her. Abby leaned over and put her arms around his waist and her head on his back. "Why are you acting jealous? I chose you, remember? I wouldn't go back on that, not without talking to you first about it. And I don't want to."

He turned in her arms and wrapped his arms around her. "Sorry. I don't know why either. I guess I shouldn't be. I mean I heard the way you guys talked about him sometimes and it was like you had him up on a pedestal of Peter Priesthoodiness or something, and I'd think, 'Is that what she expects from me?' That's just not me."

"You feel like that because you don't hear the way I talk about you," Abby said, looking up at him. "Used to drive him crazy. It's why he's so frosty towards you. He knows how I feel about you, and he also knew he couldn't compete."

Will looked down on her, a smile on his face. "You're just saying that."

"Nope, not a bit," Abby said, smiling back.

He kissed her softly. She sighed as his touch swirled her head and his arms held her tightly against him. She was in heaven being kissed by the only angel she'd ever dreamed about. She was glad she sat on the couch because his lips managed to turn her knees to jelly as sighs escaped her throat.

"Do that all the time. I'll never, ever get tired of it," she said as he pulled away.

"Better not," he said, leaving a burning trail of heat along her forehead as he swept some of her hair to the side and behind her ear.

She made to move over so he could sit next to her but he turned to the TV.

"Want to watch anything specific?" he asked.

She shook her head. "Just whatever is fine. I need to email my teachers."

Almost as soon as she got comfortable, Will's phone pinged—and continued to do so all the rest of the night. Abby couldn't deny that she felt fairly ignored, but she couldn't expect Will to change the level of comfort he felt around her even if he'd decided to take their relationship to the next level. Comfortable was good . . . right?

CHAPTER 19

Sara knocked on Abby's door.

"Come in." She could hear her sister's voice from the other side.

"Hey," Sara said as she opened the door. "I'm going to make pancakes this morning. Want some?"

"Yeah, I'll hobble out to the kitchen."

"You sure?" Sara asked. "I can bring them to you."

"Nah, I'm getting sick of laying around and I have to get used to these crutches."

Sara was halfway through the pancake batter when Abby joined her.

"Can I ask you a question that I hope you don't get mad at me for?" Abby asked.

"Okay," Sara said.

"Have you heard from Brandon in the last couple of days?"

"Yes. He sent me a text yesterday."

"And?"

"And he's sad, but he's doing okay."

"Oh. What about Evan?"

Sara looked at her sister. "Nope. Nothing since a couple of weeks ago. I tried last week and once more the day you broke your ankle, but he never returned them."

"I'm sorry, Sara. I wonder what's up with him."

Sara shrugged. "I don't know. I wish I knew. He was really upset. I could tell he was but he was trying to hide how much from me. Brandon hasn't even really heard from him either and they've gotten to be good friends recently."

Abby sighed. "This sucks."

"I know," Sara said, bringing the finished stack over to the table. She got tableware for them both and, after praying over the food, plated out the pancakes. "I probably forgot to tell you amongst all the drama, but he said something really weird right before he took me home that last day. He said that he had to tell me about something that happened down at ASU. And he kept telling me he wished things were different, but then the phone call came in and he never finished his thought."

"I wonder what he was talking about."

"Don't know. He'd been talking about wanting to be Brandon Sanderson."

Abby laughed. "Who?"

"You know, the writer. He wrote all those fantasy books and he also teaches at BYU. I guess Evan wants to be a writer too, and he'd rather teach English than do whatever it is his family expects him to do."

"Oh. Yeah, I wonder if he was talking about his graduate work. Maybe he's decided but he doesn't really want to do it, but feels he has to."

"Maybe, but he was just so upset. Seemed like it was more than that."

"Huh. I mean, how sad is that? Why can't his family accept what he wants to do? Why wouldn't you want your child to be happy?"

"Maybe they think he'd be happier doing what they think he should be doing?"

"I'm glad Mom and Dad never thought like that," Abby sniffed. "They would have been happy if we'd decided to be sanitation workers or waitresses if that's the kind of job we wanted."

"I know, but they were awesome parents, and not everyone's parents think like they did," Sara said. "It's times like this that I really miss them. It would be nice to be able to talk to them about all of this stuff."

Abby put down her fork. "I know. I was just thinking the same thing."

Sara's phone beeped. She pulled it out from under her seat.

"It's Evan!" she cried. "He wants to make sure I'll be at church today. Says he wants to talk to me." Her smile was so huge it almost hurt her face.

"Yay!" Abby said, clapping her hands. "Finally. Let's get going so we can get you ready."

"It's not like I'm getting ready for prom or something," Sara said, giving her sister a look.

"Right, but it doesn't hurt to look extra scrumptious after he hasn't seen you in a while."

Sara laughed, but she didn't disagree with her sister about that.

Sara hurried through the church doors and into the foyer. She looked around but Evan wasn't there. She'd almost made it into the chapel when Ben, one of the bishop's clerks stopped her.

"Hey, Sara, Bishop wants to know if you can stop by his office after sacrament meeting so he can talk to you," he said. "Can you?"

"Uh, yeah, sure," Sara said, impatiently. "Tell him that should be fine."

"Okay, great," he said, turning to go back into his office.

Sara wheeled into the chapel and looked over the rows of seats. Evan was nowhere in sight. She did see Brandon sitting on the back row, the one with the cutout for wheelchairs. He motioned to her when he saw her. She rolled up and parked next to him.

"Brandon, have you seen Evan?" she asked.

"No, did you hear from him?" he asked.

"Yes, this morning," she confirmed. "He wanted to make sure I was going to be at church today so we could talk."

Brandon smiled at her. "Great! He hasn't said a word to me but I haven't seen him yet." Brandon looked past her and his shoulders stiffened. Abby hobbled in on her walking boot and crutches, followed closely behind by Will. They took up the pew in front of Sara and Brandon. Abby turned around.

"Have you seen Evan?" she asked Sara, ignoring Brandon. Sara shook her head.

"They're going to be late," Will said.

"How do you know?" Abby asked.

Before Will could answer the question, Brandon tapped Sara on the arm and nodded towards the chapel doors. His face was a mask of worry and confusion. Sara turned and felt her stomach clench sickeningly.

Olivia stepped into the chapel, followed by Evan . . . holding the hand of a dark-haired girl Sara had never seen before.

Evan locked eyes with Sara. His face looked apologetic, but Sara turned away. She took deep breaths in and out, trying to keep tears from forming in her eyes. So that was what he needed to tell her about his time at ASU. She should have known. A guy as good-looking, kind, sweet and talented as Evan would not have been single for very long down there. Why not just tell her, though? Why string her along and act like he liked her and then spring something on her like this? Was this funny to him? Was this a sick joke?

"Are you okay?" Brandon whispered.

All Sara could do was shake her head and stare at her clenched hands in her lap. Before Brandon could do anything about it, the first counselor got up and started the meeting. She was able to make it through the sacrament, but then escaped to the bathroom and locked herself in a stall. She rubbed away her tears with a wad of toilet paper. Her face was hot from holding in her sobs when, a few minutes later, she heard Abby struggle her way into the room.

"Sara, can you let me in?"

She complied, but seeing her worried sister only made her tears worse.

"I'm sorry, hon," Abby said, hugging her sister. "Why didn't he just tell you? Or why didn't he just break up with her? I'm all kinds of confused right now."

"Me, too. I have no idea what's going on. Why did he need to see me here at church? Why couldn't he have just brought her by our house yesterday and introduced her so I could have done this in private? Did he really need to flaunt her and break my heart in front of the whole ward?"

Abby hugged Sara as she cried. Sara was able to get herself under control after a while and she went to the sink to splash some cold water on her face. Her makeup job was demolished but at that point she didn't care. She felt hurt, angry, and betrayed. But most of all, hopeless.

Then she found herself excusing his behavior. Evan had never said she and he were dating, or confirmed he was singling her out. It was his actions alone that implied it all the time. To his credit, he did consistently deny that they were dating. And now she knew why.

"I'm going to sit out in the foyer," Sara said. "The bishop wants to see me after sacrament. I just can't go back in there."

"Okay, I'll meet you out there after the meeting. Do you want to go home afterward?"

Sara nodded. Crawling into bed and sleeping the rest of the day away sounded really good right at that moment.

Sara paced the foyer after Abby went back into the chapel. She found she couldn't hold still. There was no need for this. If he knew he had a girlfriend back in Arizona, he should have kept Sara at arm's length instead of hanging out with her as much as possible, texting her all the time, and showing preference for her company at church and activities. All of this would have hurt less if he'd acted more like a casual acquaintance than someone who had other intentions.

He wasn't entirely at fault, she tried to reason with herself. She was just as guilty in the way she was feeling because she'd allowed herself to hope that, for once, someone she wanted her back. She'd secretly held onto the idea that someone that she admired and respected might find her interesting and attractive. But, as usual, she was deluding herself. She'd been sent straight back to the friend zone—in the most humiliating way possible.

She wandered down the hall toward the bishop's office and looked out the glass doorway at the front of the building. The grey clouds she'd barely noticed when they'd arrived now hung low over the valley. It was going to rain today. Seemed appropriate considering how desolate she felt inside. She heard the organ music begin, indicating the end of the meeting, and the varied chatter of people leaving the chapel, but she didn't turn around. She didn't want to. She'd rather not have to see Evan come back out with the raven-haired beauty he'd brought with him. She chuckled ruefully to herself. His mother must be thrilled. She looked like she belonged in the family with those tresses of dark hair and cream-colored skin. Not like Sara with her reddish hair and ghost-white, freckled complexion.

The noise of people in the foyer died down as they either left or went to Sunday School before Sara dared turn around. There, standing in front of the bishop's office staring at her, was the girl Evan had brought with her. When she saw Sara had seen her, she raised a hand in greeting.

"Hi," she said sweetly. "You're Sara, aren't you?"

To say Sara was shocked this girl knew her name was putting it mildly.

"Uh, yeah. I'm Sara Larsen," Sara said.

"Evan's told me so much about you," she said, smiling.

"Really? He hasn't told me a thing about you," Sara said.

"I'm not surprised," the girl said. "He's always been sort of private."

That logic didn't make any sense at all to Sara.

"I'm Ashley Beckett," she said, coming up to Sara. "I'm Evan's girlfriend."

Sara swallowed. "It's, um, nice to meet you, Ashley. I've known Evan since high school."

"Yeah, he was telling me. Says you play the violin. I wish I had been here that Sunday you guys played together. Evan plays the piano so beautifully. It would have been awesome to see it. But I was busy with family stuff and, well, if we're being honest, Evan and I were taking a *break*, at the time, if you know what I mean."

A break. No she didn't know what she meant. To her, that sounded like they'd broken up, but if that was the case, what had changed?

"I mean, I feel like I know you already between Evan and Olivia. It's almost like we're already friends. I hope that's okay with you. I mean, I don't want to push myself on people, but they both say you're so nice and sweet and I can totally see that already."

Sara tried to give Ashley a half-hearted smile. "One can't have too many friends, right?"

"Right!" Ashley said. "I'm going to be visiting for a few weeks while we get things worked, so I'd love to have people I can hang out with besides those that are potentially going to be family."

"You mean—?"

Ashley sat down on one of the chairs outside the bishop's office. She leaned into Sara.

"Don't say anything, okay?" Ashley said in a conspiratorial voice. "But I think Evan's pretty close to, you know, popping the question. It's been a long time coming, but I think he's finally ready now."

Sara had to swallow harder now to keep tears from popping up in her eyes. "Oh. He hadn't mentioned anything to me, but if that's the case, that should be exciting."

"I know. I'm so thrilled. Knowing him, it's bound to be a big, romantic surprise."

Sara bit her lip almost to the point of drawing blood—the thought of Evan asking this girl to marry him the way Sara had envisioned him asking *her* . . .

"I don't want to come across as nosey or rude. Forgive me for asking, but what made you guys get back together after your break?" Sara asked.

Ashley's face fell a little for the first time since their conversation started. "I, uh, I don't know if I should say anything."

"Oh, is it personal? I'm sorry. I shouldn't have pried."

"Well, it's just that—I have to be honest with you—I was watching you with your sister today during church. I'm a little jealous. I don't have any siblings. I'm an only child. I always wished I had some, which is why I'm excited that when Evan and I marry, I'll be getting a sister finally. It must be nice to have someone to confide in. Sometimes there are things you need to tell someone, and you certainly don't want to tell your parents."

"Oh, yeah, I guess that could be true."

"Do you . . . do you mind if I tell you something? You have to promise not to say anything to anyone—even your sister, or Evan? He would kill me if he knew, but I really, really need to tell someone. Sometimes I feel like I'll explode if I can't share it."

Sara held her breath. With her going on like this, she wasn't sure she wanted to know now. A pit of dread formed in her stomach.

"I promise I won't say anything to anyone."

Ashley smiled in relief. "Thank you. You don't know how happy this makes me. I've been carrying this around on my own, even without Evan's help for a while. I mean, I've been talking to my bishop and all, but sometimes that's almost as bad as talking to your parents. But you have to do what you have to do when you love someone."

Sara wished that Ashley would get to the point because the longer she went on the worse the pit in her stomach got.

"So, Evan and I had been dating for a few months. And we really liked each other. Like, *really* liked each other, and, well, things got a little heated one night and we sort of, kind of . . . messed up."

Sara's stomach dropped altogether.

"We agreed to take some time apart, but I stayed in contact because, well, we didn't want to take the chance that I might be, you know, pregnant. We didn't use protection or anything."

Sara nodded her head because she didn't have any words to say.

"Please, Sara, you can't say a word to anyone. I don't want this to get around the ward. It was bad enough that rumors were flying around the school ward down in Arizona. That's why Evan came home. It was just too much for him to know that people were talking about him behind his back, like he was a bad person or something, for making one mistake. I don't want people here to think that. He's not; we just loved each other too much to be prudent and, well, marriage will solve any further complications."

"I can understand that," Sara said, her voice gruffer than she would have liked it to be. "I won't say anything. Making a mistake, even a big one, doesn't make you a bad person. That's why Jesus carried out the Atonement right?"

"Exactly," Ashley said. "I'm so glad you understand. I knew you would."

Abby came up behind the two women. "Are you ready to go home?"

"Not yet," Sara said. "The bishop wants to see me but I guess he's talking to Evan first. Abby, this is Evan's girlfriend, Ashley. Ashley, this is my sister, Abby."

"Hi!" the both of them said to the other. At that moment the door to the bishop's office opened and Evan stepped out into a trio of expectant eyes.

"Oh, hi, ladies," Evan said, markedly more nervous than he was half a second ago.

"Hi, Evan," Sara said. "I'm sorry, I don't have time to talk today. The bishop needs to see me. Ashley tells me you both have a busy schedule for the next week or two, so don't worry about . . . whatever you needed to discuss."

Evan looked like he wanted to say something but Ashely grabbed his arm and steered him towards the foyer. "Let's see if we can catch the last part of class."

Abby gave Sara a questioning look.

"I'm ready, Bishop," Sara said, rolling into his office and shutting the door.

CHAPTER 20

Abby sat on the couch texting Will. She looked occasionally towards Sara's bedroom and stared at it.

Will, I'm really worried about Sara

How is she

She's not doing well
she's been in her room crying since church

She needs to get over Evan
what a douchebag thing to do

Easier said than done

I know but it will be better for her

Maybe I should have Brandon come over and talk to her
they're friends

Why would you do that?
You want him to come over so you can see him, don't you?□
You're already starting up with this stuff?

What are you talking about?
I'm not starting anything

Where are you anyway
I thought you'd come over right after church but I haven't seen you yet

I'm busy doing something for my mom
I'll be over in a little while
What do you want to do this week?
I know it's hard to do stuff with your foot

I have to get some homework done so if you have stuff you need to do this week just get it done
don't worry about me

I always worry about you

Awww you're so sweet
that's one of the reasons I love you

You do?
You love me?

Yes, you nerd brain, I've said it before

Oh, I guess it just feels different now

I guess it would, wouldn't it
it's true though

I got to go, my mom's trying to get my attention☐
I'll come over in a while

Ok, see you later

Abby put her phone down. She was really tempted to get up and knock on her sister's door, but she knew Sara didn't want to talk right now. It wasn't that she didn't trust Abby, it was just that sometimes Sara liked to work things out by herself. Still, she usually cried it out for a while and then got control of herself. This time, she'd been crying for several hours and Abby was starting to worry she'd make herself sick. She thought about calling Crystal. But Crystal wasn't a mellow personality like their mother had been and Sara probably wouldn't respond well to her brand of mothering.

Sara's door opened and she wheeled herself across the hall to the bathroom, sniffling, not even looking at Abby. Abby didn't know what to do for her. Sara's reaction felt stronger than it should be for getting over a simple crush, but when she'd asked her about it, Sara wouldn't say a word about what was going on.

Abby clenched her fists. She knew something fishy was going on when she came up to Sara and she was talking to that girl Evan dragged in to church—*Ashley*. Ashley seemed much too calm and smug for Abby's tastes. She must have said something to Sara, but, for whatever reason, Sara wasn't willing to tell her what.

She picked her phone back up and texted Brandon.

> *I know you don't want to talk to me right now, but I'm really worried about Sara.*
> *Could you please come over and talk to her?*
> *She's really hurting and she won't talk to me about it. Maybe you can get her to talk to you?*
> *Please?*

She closed her eyes and pressed the Send button. She hoped Brandon was a big enough guy to realize that this had nothing to do with Abby, and everything to do with her sister.

Her phone buzzed.

I'll be right over. Do you think she'll want a blessing?

Abby let out a relieved sigh.

> *Yes, I think she would if you offered her one. Thank you.*

Abby stood up and put her phone in her pocket. She felt tears drip down her face. Now that she was dating Will, there was a small part of her that regretted how she'd ended things with Brandon. It wasn't that she regretted choosing Will, but that, over and over, Brandon had proven what a good guy he was and how much of a good thing they could have had . . . if Will hadn't put himself forward like he had finally.

She threw some frozen chicken in a baking dish, and dumped some spices over them with some butter when the doorbell rang. She hobbled over to get it. Brandon stood there, still in his church clothes.

"Thank you," she said, as she moved out of the way to let him in. "I know I already said it, but I really do mean it."

"I know. I'll go see if she'll talk to me," he said, brushing past her.

She bit her lip as he walked by her. She couldn't blame him for not wanting to talk to her. She made her way back to the kitchen, put some water on to boil, and started peeling potatoes. By the time the potatoes were softened, drained, and run through the mixer for mashed potatoes, Brandon came back into the kitchen with his hands in his pockets and his head down.

"She didn't really tell me what was going on besides what we already knew, but she did want the blessing, so I gave her one," he sighed. "Has she been like that since church?"

Abby nodded. "Yeah. Something about her reaction doesn't sit right with me. It's stronger than if it were just that she found out her crush had a girlfriend. So, hear me out, this is what I've been thinking–*if* Evan really does like my sister like we thought—even though he never said anything out loud—and *if* the only problem was that he had a girlfriend back in college, then you'd think that the problem would be easily solved by breaking up with the girlfriend, right?"

Brandon nodded. "He never told me he had a girlfriend, or even that he'd dated anyone in Arizona.. He only ever talked about Sara."

"That's why this is so weird," Abby said. "I mean, if they dated a couple of times, and then he left her there and came home, and never talked about her, so you'd think he was thinking they'd broken up. In that case, it's easy to see how she might have misinterpreted his intentions. Some guys are just like that—they don't like to do the dirty work of breaking up with someone so they just leave. But this girl acts like nothing had changed. Maybe he didn't really break up with her, but he meant to. What a mess."

"No doubt," Brandon said. "But I think you're right—something's off about the whole thing. It seems like there's more to it than just that. Even if it took her a week and a half to travel to Salt Lake, she's been here long enough for Evan to break up with her before they came to church. Why not do it before they walked through the door and do that to Sara? Or why not call Sara and tell her what was about to happen?"

"Well, he may have tried to. She got a text from him on Saturday asking if she'd be in church on Sunday so they could talk. Maybe he thought he'd get there early so they could talk before church started and he wouldn't have to make a scene, but things didn't work like they were supposed to."

"That still doesn't sound right," Brandon said. "I can tell you he cared about Sara. I was pretty sure if it wasn't love, it was pretty close to it. You don't do something like that to someone you care about that much. You don't spring something like that in public, even if you think you'll be mostly alone. You wouldn't want to risk having witnesses to something so private." He rubbed his face with his hands. "At least *you* were smart enough to tell me in private." He held up his hand when Abby opened her mouth to say something. "I really don't want to revisit that—I'm just saying, this just doesn't seem like something Evan would do."

A knock came at the door.

"That's probably Will," Abby said, hobbling over to the door.

"Then I probably better get going," Brandon said. "Let me know if Sara needs me to come over again. I have to work tomorrow but anytime after work I'm free."

Abby nodded and tried to give him a smile before she opened the door.

"Thanks again, Brandon," she said, opening the door.

Will's look of surprise at seeing Brandon walk past him through the door turned to irritation as he came into the house.

"Wow," he said, rounding on Abby. "Seriously?"

"What?" Abby said, going back into the kitchen to finish her dinner.

"You just couldn't help yourself, could you?" he said, his arms folded.

"You're going to have to do a lot better than that, Will," Abby said, throwing the bag of vegetables in the microwave.

"Are you really that insecure that you just have to surround yourself with guys who adore you?" Will said. "Didn't I ask you not to contact him?"

Abby's eyes zeroed in on Will's face and put her fist on her hip. "Excuse me, but since when did you become my boss?"

"Since it's only courtesy to respect your boyfriend's wishes," he said.

"That," she said, pointing to the front door, "had nothing to do with me. I had him come over because he and Sara are friends and he offered to give Sara a priesthood blessing."

"Which I could have done just as well had you asked me," Will said.

"Really?" Abby accused. "Since when? I've never even seen you pass the sacrament, nor have I seen you take a single one of your priesthood responsibilities seriously. Why would I assume you were able to? Which is actually beside the point. Sara wouldn't have wanted one from you anyway. She likes you fine but she wouldn't have trusted you enough to ask you for one."

Will sniffed and turned away from her. "I see how it is. Is that the way you feel, then? Am I not worthy enough for you?"

Abby let out a long-suffering sigh. "Will, why are we fighting about this? I just wanted you to come over so we could have dinner and hang out."

"Well, now that I know a little about how you really feel about me, I'm curious to know everything."

"Will, come on," Abby said, sitting down on a dining room chair. "Have I ever once, in the whole time we've known each other, asked you to prove your worthiness to me? No. Why? Because I don't care. That's your business. Not mine. Does it affect how I feel about you? No. I care about you because there's more than one thing that makes you important to me. If you struggle with worthiness, then I'm here to support you if you need it. If you don't, great. We'll just move forward. Is that what you're trying to say?"

"No!" he said. "I don't even know what we're fighting about anymore either, except for the fact that I get here planning on spending some alone time with you and I find Brandon here."

Abby rolled her eyes. "Like I said, he was here for Sara! He wasn't planning on staying and he barely said four sentences to me before he walked into her room."

"You're so full of it," he said. "Like he'd just pass up the chance to talk to you."

"Will, what is the matter with you? You think I'm lying to you? Why would I do that?"

"I don't know, you tell me," he said, heading towards the door. "Nothing to say?"

He yanked the door open.

"I don't even know what the problem is or why you think I'm lying to you," she said, on the verge of tears. "I don't understand where this jealousy is coming from."

"Then maybe I should give you some time to think about it," he said, "If you seriously can't see it."

He went out the door and slammed it behind him.

"What is going on out here?" Sara said, coming out into the front room as Abby sank down to the couch, hands covering her face.

"I don't know," Abby said through tears. "He comes in here and loses it because Brandon was here and accuses me of lying to him about Brandon. I tried to tell him he was here for you but he didn't believe me and stormed out of here. I don't get it. What is wrong with all the guys around here?"

Sara came up to her sister and put her arms around her and they cried together. "I don't know either. Seems like the only sane ones right now are the bishop and Brandon."

Abby couldn't help but chuckle a little through her tears. "Then maybe just the bishop because Brandon hates my guts right now."

"He doesn't hate your guts," Sara said. "He's just licking his wounds right now. He really liked you."

"He told you that?"

Sara sniffed. "No. You think he'd honestly say something like that to the sister of the person he liked? I just know."

"It doesn't matter," Abby said. "Even if it's true, I still want to be with Will even if he's being an idiot right now."

Sara rolled her eyes and sighed. "What else is new?"

CHAPTER 21

Abby nearly threw her cell phone on the floor for the eightieth time that week. She'd sent yet another text to Will to meet up with him at her house to ride to activity night at the ward, but she hadn't heard from him since morning. He'd agreed to it, then she hadn't heard from him the rest of the day. It'd been happening like that all week since their argument on Sunday. In fact, she hadn't seen him in person since then even though he was supposed to go with her to register for classes for the next semester.

She got in her car and dialed Sara's number.

"Hey, where are you?" she asked her sister.

"I'm over at Brandon's," Sara said. "He got some stuff in the mail today and wanted my help putting it up before we came to the activity."

"So he'll drive you then?"

"Yeah, he'll take me. I'll see you over there, then you can take me home."

"Okay, I'm heading over now, then."

She drove over to the church, careful to follow all the traffic laws. If she hadn't been so mindful, she might have gotten a ticket with how angry she felt. Will was going to get a piece of her mind when she found him. He wasn't going to like it, but she didn't care. He didn't get to throw a tantrum and ghost her just because of his weird, jealous fascination with Brandon. She should have told him that if she wanted to hang out with Brandon, then she would whether Will liked it or not, but that would have only made the argument worse. This brattiness was not going to fly with her. She wondered if this was the reason his relationships never lasted long. She'd always assumed it was because he liked catch and release. He'd never bring his dates around her—at the time it was a relief because she didn't like having to be the third wheel, but now it made her wonder if it was the reason she'd missed this part of his personality.

She pulled up to the church and tilted her head to the side. All the front windows were dark. There was a lot going on in the building, so the fact that it was dark was weird. She got out of the car and struggled up the stairs. She tried the doors and they were unlocked. She shrugged. Probably some kids playing with the lights.

When she entered the foyer, none of the lights in that part of the building were on, including the cultural hall. But at the end of the hallway were a couple of rooms with lights on and their doors open. She made her way towards the rooms, but slowed as she neared because she could hear voices coming from them. Just as she reached the door, she recognized the voices.

"I don't know what game you're playing, but I'm tired of it." Olivia's voice rang clearly through the open door.

"I don't know what you're talking about." And that was Will's voice.

Abby gasped. Will was in there with Olivia. She gritted her teeth but waited to hear what they were talking about.

"Oh, just that Emily keeps seeing your car parked at Abby's house all the time these days," Olivia accused.

"And that's different from any other time?" Will defended.

"Humph, I just think it's awfully convenient that you disappear on me during the week and then you show up at my door when you feel like it, and act like nothing is wrong," she said.

Abby bit her lip. What? He was going over to Olivia's? For what?

"You're imagining things," he said. "I'm not treating you any differently than normal. You're the one that insists on weekends because you have school during the week. And lately you haven't even been available then either. What, do you expect me to be on call?"

"That might be nice for once," she said. "At least I'd know I could count on you. For all I know, you could be dating Abby with as much time as you spend with her."

"Why would I be dating Abby when I'm getting ready to propose to you?"

Abby sucked in a breath. For a moment, she felt like she was going to pass out.

"Besides, you know I'm not attracted to girls like her—she has too much fluff. Can't get a good grip around the middle to hold them close. Like this." A silence overtook the room before Abby could take control over her breathing again.

She surged forward and slammed the door open wide and watched in horror as she found Will kissing Olivia quite deeply.

"Like what, Will?" Abby demanded. "Like that, you mean? You couldn't hold me like that? Because you couldn't possibly be dating me, or kissing me, or telling me that you want to try *us* for a while?"

Olivia stood up straight, but instead of getting mad at Will, she smirked at Abby.

"Wow, talk about desperate," Olivia said. "You actually thought he was talking about dating you? That's cute. Or was that just what you wanted to believe. You always did follow him around like a puppy in high school."

Abby ignored Olivia and stared straight at Will. "Well, Will? What is it?"

He didn't say anything.

Abby's lip curled. "And you called me a liar. You accused me of looking elsewhere. You are such a scumbag. I can't believe I was such a fool. What, you couldn't stand to see me happy with someone else?"

"Abby—"

"Don't. Bother!" Abby said, backing up. "Don't talk to me. Don't try to follow me. Don't you even try to touch me or I will hurt you. I hate you."

She spun around as fast as she could without falling over and hurried to her car. She nearly tripped once or twice as she struggled to get down the carpeted hallway with tears obscuring her vision. She managed to get into her car and drive several blocks before she wondered where she was going. She couldn't go home. Will might try to follow her there. She didn't want to talk to him or even look at him. He made her sick. She felt like such an idiot. She had nowhere to go, nowhere to land. Her parents were gone and she didn't know where to turn now that her world was falling apart.

She wiped her face with the back of her hand. Where was her sister? She needed Sara. Sara would understand. Sara loved her. She was the only person in the whole world that loved her for who she was, good and bad. And she needed to be with someone who loved her like that. Her anguished brain tried to think straight. Sara was at Brandon's. Abby did not want to go there, but she needed her sister. She didn't want to go home and be alone.

She steered her car towards Brandon's house. She parked her car in front and took a deep breath. She looked a mess, and felt like it too. She couldn't help that. She'd have to let Brandon see her like this. Brandon would have never done this to her. The thought only made her cry harder. She felt twice the fool. She'd traded away something great for a cheap imitation, just to fulfill a childish fantasy. To accept a gift without wondering why it was being given after being denied her for years before that.

She struggled up the stairs to Brandon's front door and knocked. Hiccups escaped, but she endeavored to get them under control.

"Hi, I didn't think you'd be over. Sara said—" Brandon began before he saw the condition she was in. "Come in," he said, grabbing her arm and helping her into the house.

CHAPTER 22

Sara looked at the diagram and up at the wall Brandon wanted to hang the pictures on. She'd had him move his couch over so she could help him measure where each picture would hang to make up the attractive display. The sound of a car braking outside pulled Brandon away to the window.

"It's Abby," he said. "I wonder what she wants. You were supposed to meet her there, right?"

"Yes," Sara said, scrunching her eyebrows together. "Guess we'll find out."

A knock came at the door. Brandon answered, but before he got very far in his welcome, he was assisting a hysterical Abby into the house.

"Abby!" Sara said, rushing up to her sister and wrapping her arms around her. "What's wrong?"

"I . . . I heard them talking, Sara," Abby choked out. "Will and Olivia. They . . . they're dating . . . and he's going to ask her to . . . to marry him." She could barely get words out before she leaned over her lap and started to sob again.

"What? Will's dating Olvia?" Sara asked, confused. "He's supposed to be dating you. What is going on?"

"I don't know," Abby said, still bent over. "I went to the church and heard them talking. He kissed her. Told her he couldn't ever date someone like me."

"I should get you home," Sara said.

"No," Abby said, reaching out to hold her sister's arms. "I can't go home. What if he comes over to talk to me? I don't want to talk to him. I don't want to see him. Please, Sara."

Sara looked up at Brandon. He'd been silent the whole time Abby had been talking. His face was heavy.

"I . . . um, Brandon, she's in no condition to drive and I don't have my car here. Is there somewhere she can lie down for a minute?"

He seemed to shake himself out of his troubled stupor. "Oh, right, yeah," he said, standing up straighter. "Let me take you to the guest bedroom. She can lie down there. I think Colin's bed's a little too small for her."

He went over to Abby and squatted down next to her. "Abby, can I take you to the guest room?"

She looked up at him with her tear-streaked face and nodded. "I'm picking you up. I'm not going to have you try to stumble through the carpet and have you break your ankle again."

Sara's heart warmed as she watched her friend lift her sister up out of the chair and cradle her against his chest. Abby rested her head on his shoulder and held him around his neck with her free arm. For just a moment, she saw Brandon's face soften towards her sister before walking down the hallway to the bedrooms. She followed.

Brandon was still in love with Abby, though Sara had a feeling he wouldn't be in too much of a rush to admit it after she'd dumped him so unceremoniously. It had brought back all the pain of his divorce. Since Evan left, she and Brandon had had a lot of time to talk. Brandon was a really good guy. He'd probably still be married right now if his wife had been willing to work on their marriage. He wasn't one to give up on things he felt were important. But he also wasn't a masochist. He'd walked away with grace even though he still cared about his ex, and it had hurt him more than he liked to admit.

He laid Abby on the bed and pulled the throw blanket over as she sniffed. "I'll just be out there if you guys need anything. If you need me to take you home, just ask."

"Okay, thanks," Sara said. "I'll let you know. She probably just needs a minute or two."

He nodded, and looked Abby over one more time before he shut the door most of the way.

"He's so nice," Abby said in a scratchy voice. "It's a wonder you haven't started dating him."

Sara laughed. "We joked about that one time. We agreed that it might have been possible if not for one really big problem."

"What's that?" Abby said, turning over.

"We're both in love with someone else," Sara said.

"You may be still, but he's not," Abby said.

"I think you're wrong but, like I said, I don't know for sure," Sara said. "He's never come out and said it, but I bet I'm right."

"Doesn't matter, Sara," Abby said. "I'm a big idiot. I'm not saying I didn't love Will. I do. Did. I don't know what I am with him. I just hurt. You should have heard what he said." A new set of tears came rolling down her cheeks. "He said I was too 'fluffy' for him to hold me around the waist."

"Oh, Abby, I'm sorry," Sara said. "That's a terrible thing for him to say."

"How many years have I wanted to be with him; wanted him to want me? And all this time I knew exactly why he didn't. What made me think any of that had changed? What made me think I could compete with Olivia?"

"That's not the question, Abby," Sara said, holding Abby's hand. "A better question is why did he made you feel you had to compete? If he truly cared about you the way he should have, even as a friend, you wouldn't have to compete with anyone. A true friend would love you just the way you are. The size of your clothes wouldn't matter, or whether you're in a wheelchair, or if you have money or not. He would see you as the Lord sees you—beautiful and precious and funny and hard-working and strong and all the other good adjectives that make you the best Abby in the whole world. Well, at least to me."

"That's how Evan should have seen you."

"Yes, Evan should have," Sara said. "He should have been dealing in honesty and integrity, independence and forthrightness. Someone I could count on, like I always count on the Lord, to have my best interests at heart."

Abby threw her head back on her pillow. "It's so frustrating! It's frustrating that we have to let this Ashley girl have Evan," Abby said.

"She had first claim on him," Sara said. "He shouldn't have singled me out if he was committed to somebody else."

"Well, if he was so committed to her, like Ashley said he was, then why didn't he ever talk about her? Why leave her in Arizona to come here without her?"

"I don't know," Sara said. "I only know that I can't get in the way of something that happened before I was involved. If I were her, I'd expect the same."

Abby turned over so she faced the window displaying the darkness outside. "I'm so tired of all this crap, Sara."

"I know. Me, too," Sara sighed. They sat there silently for a while until Sara heard Abby's breathing had evened out. It was probably best. She needed the rest. She'd help Brandon with the rest of the picture wall and then have him take them home. Then they'd try to forget all about stupid Will and poor-judgement Evan.

Sara tried not to let her chin quiver when she thought of him, but the disappointment was still so keen. She put her head in her hand and thought back to the conversation she'd had with Ashley and felt sick once again. It wasn't the fact that Evan had messed up that made her sick. It was the rest of their conversation, and the secret she'd been sworn to. People *would* judge Evan if they knew. It was something that always bothered her. Of course you were supposed to wait until marriage, but did some people in the Church really have to treat young people like lepers just because they got caught up in a moment? Did there have to be whispers behind a couple's backs when they got married by a bishop first, instead of in the temple? It was all so stupid.

Sara got control of her emotions, smoothed her shirt out and had reached to open the bedroom door when she heard a knock at Brandon's front door. She hadn't heard anyone drive up to the house. Maybe it was Will. She stayed in the room and turned the light off and waited. If it *was* Will, she would *not* allow him in the room to upset her sister more than he already had. Sara doubted Brandon would let him get that far, but she wasn't about to take the chance. She listened at the crack in the door.

"Brother Majors, how are you this evening?" The voice of Bishop Gold came from the front room.

"Good. Welcome, Bishop, and you too, Evan," Brandon said, though it sounded like Brandon said Evan's name a little more loudly for Sara's benefit.

Sara gasped. Evan was here. What was he doing? She felt frozen at the door.

"So, Brandon, I'm wondering if you might be willing to help me with a temporary problem," the older man said.

"Whatever I can do, I'd be happy to," Brandon said.

"Brother Farris here came to me this evening with some fairly distressing news. Since it's his to tell, I'll let him apprise you of it so he can give you whatever details he wants to."

"So, the long and short of it is, my parents kicked me out of the house," Sara could hear Evan say. Her hand went to her mouth. "I don't have a job and I don't have a place to live. I just graduated with my undergrad in English from ASU a couple of months ago and I was supposed to be applying for graduate school but we disagreed on what kind of program. I finally stood up for myself tonight and told them I wouldn't be doing anything like politics or law. They basically told me I had a choice: have them choose my graduate degree and pay for it—plus living expenses—or they cut me off completely—starting now. I chose to decide my own life, but obviously that poses a huge problem right now." Sara could actually hear Evan sigh.

"What about your fiance?" Brandon asked.

"My what?" Evan asked.

"The girl, Ashley, you brought to church on Sunday. She told Sara you guys were getting engaged."

"She said what?" Evan's voice rose.

Tears immediately sprouted in Sara's eyes.

"We were never engaged. I never planned on asking her to marry me. I'm not even sure how she ended up in Riverton, let alone at my parents' house. I assume she got a hold of Olivia and Olivia helped her. We dated. That's all. I even broke up with her before I left Arizona."

Evan paused and Brandon interrupted the silence with, "Wow. That's crazy."

More silence. Then Evan said, "She told Sara we were engaged? And Sara believed her!"

"She really didn't have any reason not to," Brandon scolded. "You walked into church holding the girl's hand."

"Argh. I've made a mess of things," Evan said. "Ashley grabbed my hand right before we walked in. I had no idea Sara would be sitting right there. Then she wouldn't talk to me so I could explain."

"Gentlemen, let's get back on track, shall we?" Bishop Gold said.

"Right, sorry. Man, I need to get hold of Sara somehow," Evan said. "But I need to ask you something before I do. Could I stay here for a week or two so I can get back on my feet again? I'll try to get a job right away so I can get a place to live. My parents might be willing to give me some money for an apartment as long as I get a job."

"Man, you can stay here as long as you need to, as long as you don't mind the occasional visit from my son," Brandon said. "It's just me in this big old house."

"No, I like kids. Thank you so much. I really appreciate it."

"Well, it sounds like the living arrangements are taken care of," the bishop said. "Let me know if you need a food order while you're waiting for your first check and we'll get you taken care of."

"Bishop, don't worry about that either," Brandon said. "I got this. So, do you need anything? The guest bedroom has a bed already."

When Evan spoke, she could barely hear him. "Man, she must hate me."

"I wouldn't say that," Brandon said. "Be right back."

She tried to push forward to open the door but she felt frozen. Tears dripped down her cheeks but she couldn't lift her hand to brush them away. Her whole body trembled. Could she go out there with Evan still there? She wasn't sure if she had the strength. A shadow fell across the crack in the door and she looked up into Brandon's smiling face. He flipped on the light.

"I'm assuming you heard everything?" he said quietly.

Sara nodded.

"I think you should go out there and talk to him," he said. "I think he needs you right now. It's obvious he misses you."

"Brandon, I—I'm so---. . . ."

He reached down and gave her a hug. "You're so what?"

"Confused."

"No you're not," he said, grinning. "Go talk to him. I'll stay with Abby. She's asleep anyway, right? Go!"

With shaking arms, she rolled down the hallway until she saw Evan sitting on the couch with his head in his hands. His shoulders shook a little like he was crying. She rolled up to him, reached out, and touched his shoulder. "Evan?"

His head whipped up. When he saw her, he surged forward and put his arms around her. "I'm so sorry. I'm sorry you had to go through this."

She gently pushed away from him. "I know. I heard everything you said just now."

He sighed as he ran a hand through his dark hair. "Ashley is not my fiance. We were never engaged. I was never going to ask her to marry me. I don't know why she told you that."

"I do," Sara said quietly. "She said you guys made a mistake when you were dating. She said she might be pregnant."

He sucked in a breath. He searched her face for a moment and she saw a tear form at the corner of his eye. "We did. Once, right before graduation. I thought I was in control but I wasn't. She wanted to keep dating but I couldn't. I couldn't. I broke down and saw the bishop. He and I both thought it would be good to put some distance between myself and Ashley. Since I had to decide on graduate school anyway, I decided to come home for the summer. I broke up with her and came to my parents' house."

"They, if you were single, why did you keep insisting we weren't dating?"

"Because I wasn't worthy. I had stuff to work through and I didn't want to drag you through all of that. If we just called it friends, then you'd be spared. You can't believe how terrible it was down in Arizona. Somehow, everyone found out about Ashley and me and the gossip was everywhere. They'd whisper behind our backs as we walked into church. I didn't want people talking about you and making you feel bad if someone happened to find out."

"Evan, I wouldn't have cared. People already stare at me and say negative things about me. I mean, it's not the same thing, but I don't care what people think about me. Well, everyone except for you and my sister. I mean, it's sweet that you wanted to protect me from that, but I'm stronger than I look. The only thing I care about is whether you are a good person, and you are, Evan."

"Well, I'm super poor and a huge failure at the moment," Evan said.

Sara grabbed his hands. "So what if you're poor? What does that have to do with anything? And you're only a failure if you give up. Are you going to give up on school and just work?"

"I don't want to, but I don't see what choice I have," he said.

"What about student loans?"

"I don't know the first thing about those," Evan said, his cheeks coloring a little. "My parents always paid for everything."

Sara reached out and touched her hand to his cheek. "Do you want to keep going to school?"

"Yes."

"And do what?"

"What we talked about before," he said, looking into her eyes. "I want to teach college English, or high school maybe."

"And you still want to write?"

He nodded.

"Where do you want to go to school?"

"Anywhere that will accept me," he said. "Or anywhere that will work around my work schedule—when I get a job."

Sara smiled at him. "Okay, that's a plan we can work with."

"We?"

"Well, yes. Unless you don't want my help."

He grabbed her hand off his face and squeezed it. "No, I want your help. I've missed you so much. I didn't realize how much until I was sitting at my parents' house between Olivia and Ashley and everyone was sitting there talking over me about *my* future. And all I could think of was that you're the only one who's ever been willing to listen to what I wanted. The only one who actually thought what I wanted had value. That's why I couldn't do it. Why I stood up to them finally. Because of you."

Tears leaked out of Sara's eyes. "I'm so glad you stood up for yourself. I know that was probably a hard thing to do."

"It was worth it, though," Evan said. "Do you know what happened when my parents kicked me out? Ashley broke up with me." He laughed.

"I thought you broke up with her before you left Arizona?"

"Yes!" Evan said, continuing to laugh. "She took a pregnancy test when we were still together, and it was negative. So I figured I'd dodged a bullet and I didn't need anymore temptation. I broke up with her, but she followed me here. Tonight, when she heard I wasn't getting any more family money, she said she was glad she wasn't pregnant, that I was selfish for wanting to run my own life, and then she stormed out."

"Oh, Evan," Sara said, hugging him. "So she was lying about everything."

"Yes," Evan said. "I would have never left her in Arizona pregnant and alone."

"I know!" she said. "I knew you never could have. I should have known she was lying to me. I couldn't understand why you never told me about her if you were so close to getting engaged. "

"I would have stayed away from you if I had been," Evan said into her hair. "I couldn't have done that to you, Sara. I care about you too much. You're one of the best things to have ever happened to me. I hope one day I'll be worthy of you."

"Don't say that, Evan," Sara said. "As long as you're trying to be the best you can be, I don't care. And don't do it for me. Do it for yourself."

"I am going to do it for you," he said, looking into her eyes. "Once I get my life straightened out, find a job, get back into school, I'm not going to waste any more time. I don't want to risk losing you. Sara Larson, I love you. I want you to marry me. I need to get a few things worked out but then I want to give you all the rest of it—a ring, a dress, a wedding, my worthiness."

Sara laughed. "I want all of that too, as long as it's with you. Let's just go one step at a time. I love you too, Evan. Since high school." She giggled. "It was just a crush back then, and I was too shy to say it. It's been a long wait, but I'll gladly wait a little longer if it's for you."

She grabbed him around the neck and kissed him. He held her tightly. He was the poorest guy she'd ever known but she loved him more richly than she thought possible. The best part of it was that he wanted her too. He missed her, and wanted to be by her side; wanted to be worthy of her. Even if she had to wait years, she would because he was worth the wait. But, knowing Evan, she probably wouldn't have to wait that long. She just had to be patient a bit longer. She'd be right by his side helping him every way she could.

"So are you guys getting married or what?" Brandon said, coming back into the room.

"Probably," Sara said. "He just needs a job, an education and a few other things, but then I think we'll be set."

Brandon laughed. "Well, while you were busy talking, I was poking around on my company's website and it seems there might be a job or two there that you qualify for. Probably not the most exciting work—technical writing, but if you manage to snag it, it would be close by, good pay, good benefits, and they might even help you with graduate school. They do that sometimes so they can brag that their execs have graduate degrees. I'll probably use that benefit myself someday. Hey, maybe we can ride to work together."

"Great idea. That way you'll have time to give me lessons on how to live on a paycheck."

Sara and Brandon laughed. Evan's smile in response filled up every last space in her heart.

CHAPTER 23

Abby sat at her dining room table finishing her notes for spring finals. The sun shone brightly through the curtains and she found herself staring at the light dappling the carpet. She'd lost her desire to study anymore that day.

She should have gone with Evan and Sara to the arts festival at Riverton Park but she'd declined. She knew she needed to study. What she hadn't said was that she didn't want to accidentally run into Brandon on the way there. Evan, even all these months later, was still living with Brandon. They commuted to work together, were the best of friends—with each other as well as with Sara. And since Evan and Sara were all but engaged, that left Abby in an awkward no man's land, since Brandon still wasn't talking to her.

She honestly didn't blame him. She hadn't treated him very well, and the several times she'd offered him olive branches of friendship he'd politely declined. So when Evan and Sara had invited her to go with them to the festival, she'd declined. She didn't want to get stuck wandering around alone, and certainly not alone with Brandon, or as a third wheel to Sara and Evan. None of those options were appealing. They'd assured her Brandon was out of town with his son, but she'd declined anyway. Art stuff was Sara and Evan's thing, not Abby's.

Abby's phone pinged.

There're at least three vendors here with kettle corn.
You're missing out.

That's just rude and you know it.

Just saying. And candied almonds. And no one's parked down over by the baseball diamonds hardly.

What are you trying to do to me?

Trying to bring you out of your depresso shellwe love you and want to hang out with you

I love you both too

There's a lady here selling olive oil essential oil soaps with jasmine and coconut milk

Fine, you win, you're a jerk

You love me

Abby put away her study materials and got into her car. It was a nice day for late May, and a little early for an arts festival, but, after the long winter they'd had, people wanted to get outside. She parked near the baseball diamonds, surprised she found a spot at all, and bent down to tie her shoe. They were new comfy canvas sneakers. She'd given up on heels after breaking her ankle. She looked around and sighed. This was where she and Brandon came on their first date, if you could call walking around a park a date. But it's where she first got a glimpse of the kind of person he was, a hint that she sort of did like him— and where he got bugged at how much she talked about Will. That felt like a lifetime ago instead of just last year. She hadn't heard from Will since before Christmas, *and good riddance.* Last she'd heard, he'd actually managed to convince Olivia to get engaged to him. She wasn't sure if they'd actually gotten married; Evan hadn't been invited to a wedding if one had taken place. That fact alone made Abby's blood boil on Evan's behalf. How could his family still be so angry with him enough to not invite him to an event as important as a wedding? Once they'd given him a small portion of his inheritance to set himself up, they'd shut the door in his face and never talked to him again. It was ridiculous. But he never complained, at least, not to her. She figured he was too happy being with Sara to worry about it. And for her part, Sara was in seventh heaven now that she was with Evan. She loved to see her sister so happy. They'd had enough crap in their lives to last a lifetime.

She walked past the port-a-potties to where some woman had a booth set up with all kinds of hand-quilted items for sale, a man with chainsaw-sculpted wood statues, tons of jewelry booths, and the odd painting booth.

"Dad, look over here," a boy's voice cried. "I want one of those."

"Um, no," the man said. Abby turned around. It was Brandon's voice. He stopped when he caught her eye. "Abby."

"Hi, Brandon," Abby said, a little shyly.

The little boy that came to stand up next to him looked just like the picture Brandon had showed her all those months ago. He was a little older looking, and a little cleaner but still had that same tousled brown hair and the same blue eyes his dad had.

"Hi!" he said, waving at Abby.

"Hi, Colin," Abby said, waving back.

"Dad, she knows my name," Colin said looking up at his dad shocked.

"I told it to her before," Brandon said. "This is my friend, Abby."

Friend. The word made Abby smile a little. At least she wasn't "heartless witch" or "callous female."

"How do you know my dad?" Colin asked.

"We go to the same church," Abby said. "Plus, my sister is dating Evan."

"Oh! The lady in the wheelchair," Colin said, as if that cleared everything up.

"I was on the hunt for some kettle corn," Abby said. "Do you guys want some?"

"What's kettle corn?" Colin said.

"Um, it's only the most yummy, sweetest, saltiest popcorn on the planet," Abby said.

"Yes, Dad, please? Can we go get some?"

"I guess," Brandon said, still a little wary.

"Yes!" Colin said and then grabbed Abby's hand and started pulling her through the crowd.

"My mom never lets me eat stuff like that at home. Dad doesn't care. I guess you don't either. But that sounds awesome. Do you know where it is?"

"Well, the best way to find it is to use your nose," Abby said. "It smells really good. Like candy and popcorn mixed together because that's basically what it is."

She looked back to see Brandon still following them. "Keeping up?"

"Trying," he said, speeding up to come directly up behind them. "He's quick when he wants something."

"Sort of like his dad," Abby said, smirking.

Brandon laughed. "You think so?"

"What was it? Took you all of six hours to ask me out the first time? And it was this very park, remember?"

Brandon smiled at her and his look softened. "I haven't forgotten."

"Abby, I think I found it!" Colin pointed to a booth where they had bags and bags of kettle corn already lined up in front.

"Come here, Colin. I want to show you something," Abby said, pulling Colin closer to the booth. He was just tall enough to see over the plexiglass shield to the large metal cauldron hidden behind it. "Watch what happens when they pour in more corn kernels."

The woman manning the booth took a large cup, opened the vat, and poured the kernels into the boiling oil. Immediately they were overwhelmed by the scent and sound of popping corn. Before she shut the lid, she poured in a sugar-salt mixture over the top.

"That's what gives it the salty sweetness," Abby said. "Those crystals of sugar and just a little bit of salt while the corn is popping so it melts all over the kernels."

"Want to try some?" a teen girl asked the boy holding out a plastic bin to him. Colin grabbed a small handful and popped some in his mouth.

"That is awesome!" Colin said, chomping down on the treat. "Dad, can we get some?"

"I'll get it," Abby said. "I was going to get some anyway. Then I have to find Evan and Sara. She'll just keep texting me until I do."

After buying her bag, she let Colin hold it while they walked. Over in the distance, she saw Sara's wheelchair tire peeking out of a booth. Abby flagged Sara and Evan down.

"I didn't know you were in town, Brandon," Evan said, shaking Brandon's hand.

"Michelle needed an extra day off, so Colin and I came back a day early. Heard about this and thought it would be a fun way of running off some energy after the plane ride."

"Good idea," Sara said. "Good to see you again, Colin."

"Sara, I got to meet your sister, Abby," Colin said. "She's letting me hold her kettle corn."

"Yeah, she's pretty awesome like that," Sara looked up at Abby and Brandon and how they stood together. "Hey, so, Brandon, can Evan and I steal Colin for a few minutes? There was a really cute toy booth back over there that I wanted to show him."

"Sure, you want us to stay here?"

"Nah, just wander around. We'll catch up to you," Sara said, with a twinkle in her eye.

Abby gave her sister a look but all Sara did was give her sister a smile back. They watched as the three wandered away.

"You might not get your popcorn back from Colin," Brandon said to Abby.

Abby shrugged. "It's not like I need the extra calories."

Brandon stopped and looked at her. "Abby, a lot of stuff may have been said between us, but one thing I hope you understand is that you're beautiful the way you are. You don't need to change yourself to be attractive because you already are."

"You still think I'm beautiful?" Abby said, looking at feet and biting her lip.

"Do you even need to ask that?"

"You're right. I'm sorry," she said. "You always made me feel beautiful. But I've been told—by others—in no uncertain terms that the opposite is true."

"By a moron who was trying to date two people at once, and was lying to both of them. You were the one person in his life that loved him purely and saw the good in him. If only I had been so lucky."

Abby looked up at Brandon. She'd forgotten how handsome his face was when he was sincere, or when he was saying sweet things, or any other time for that matter. But she'd blown it with him. She'd have to live with that mistake. She walked off a little ways to escape the uncomfortable direction of the conversation.

"I would have thought you'd dodged a bullet," she said, turning around to look at him. He grabbed her arm gently to stop her.

"Abby, I was mad, yes. I was hurt. But I never wanted you to drop me like you did. If you had asked me the next day to come back, I would have. You just never did. And the more I thought about it, the more mad I got. The more I saw you with that jerk, the more mad I got. And I took it out on you. I'm not proud of that. I wasted a lot of time. I think back to that night you found out about him and Olivia, and I wish I had done things differently. I should have been there for you."

"You were, though. You provided a safe place where I could rest and where I wouldn't have to face him. Plus, it had the fringe benefit of bringing Evan and Sara back together, so I can't count that night as a bad thing."

"It wasn't a bad thing—for them. Do you know how badly I just wanted to sit and hold you? But, instead, I just dropped you off on the bed."

Abby gasped and covered her mouth with her hand. She shook her head. "Do you know how badly I wanted you to stay and hold me? But I couldn't ask you to because I knew I had been so unfair."

Brandon grabbed her hand and pulled her outside of the booths to some trees that lined the edge of the parking lot. She leaned against the tree while he leaned into her with his hand braced against the tree near her head.

"I've had some very long talks with Sara," Brandon said, staring intently into her eyes, their faces so close she could feel his warm breath on her face. "And while it doesn't make it easier, I understand better why you did what you did. I wish you had listened to us so you didn't have to get so hurt. But I know you had to learn your way."

"I'd been crushing on him for so long, and we were such good friends, I thought it must be love. With you, part of me could never accept that your admiration for me was real. It didn't make sense to me. You were too nice, too thoughtful, too honest. I didn't think I deserved it. Will was my best friend, and he had never made me feel like I deserved that kind of love and respect."

"I wish I could have made you see differently," he said, putting his forehead against hers. "You are deserving of all that and more, Abby."

"I know," Abby whispered. "I wish I had seen it then. It was only after the fact that I realized how amazing you were. When there was no hope left."

"You think I'm amazing?" he asked with a crooked smirk.

"Shut up," she said. "You know you're amazing. You're an amazing man, an amazing dad, an amazing friend. Any girl would be lucky to be with you. Not sure why Michelle couldn't see that."

"Because she wasn't the one for me," he whispered back.

"Could I have another chance to, um, see if I might be?" Abby asked. "The one, you know?"

"I think I know the answer to that already, but I guess I could give you another chance . . . to see how it works out."

Abby laughed and hugged him. Then she took his face in her hands and kissed him. She had to grab onto Brandon's neck to steady herself. Her legs just didn't want to hold her up, but she didn't want to lose the feeling of his lips against hers and his arms firmly around her waist.

He tucked some hair behind her ear as he looked over her face like he was memorizing every part of it. "You are exceptionally beautiful, Abish. An apt name for a strong, faithful woman. A woman I can admire and love because I know she'll stand up for me, and stand beside me."

"Thank you, Brandon. I will always stand up for you. Now, please never, ever, ever call me by my given name again, or I will have to hurt you."

A NOTE FROM THE AUTHOR

I truly hope you enjoyed reading Date-Ability. Please consider leaving a review on the website of your choice – Amazon, Goodreads or your own social media. Reviews are like gold to an author and we appreciate them so very much!

Newsletter

Make sure to sign up for the newsletter on my website for exclusive content, upcoming release dates and other special events!

ABOUT THE AUTHOR

WS Deming loves writing romance. Her passion is fueled by binge watching BBC's "Pride and Prejudice" and "North and South" at least once a year, watching cheesy romance movies, and her ability to quote almost every 80s teen movie. She lives in a little grey house in the West Desert of Utah, referees three kids, two cats and a dog. When she's not obsessively writing something she's going to the movies, crocheting things people won't wear, and talking geek with fellow geeks.

Check out my website!